BOOK 3 OF THE SANCTUARY CHRONICLES

GATHERING

GREG RODE

ISBN: 978-1-957723-11-2

Rode. Greg
Gathering

Edited by: Melissa Long
Illustrations by: Merissa Jones

Published by Warren Publishing
Charlotte, NC
www.warrenpublishing.net
Printed in the United States

To my amazing wife, Abby. Thank you for reading all of these, especially when you like "how" I write more than "what" I write at times. I couldn't do this without you.

Don't miss the rest of The Sanctuary Chronicles by Greg Rode

Part I: Morgan

CHAPTER 1

Spring 2014

Morgan can't remember ever being so happy in her life. Windows wide open in the sparkling new Torch Red Corvette, wind blowing her already wild hair, forming an ever-shifting halo around her grinning face, she thunders east on Interstate 70 at over 100 miles an hour. The low-slung sports car simply devours the pavement, and while she'll have to stop more often for fuel at this rate of speed since gas is free and this is damn fun, she doesn't give a shit. There were many other options for her for transportation, some of which would have only forced her to stop a couple of times for gas on the seventeen-hundred-plus-mile trip, but what could be more fun, more purely American, than a cross-country trip in a red 'Vette? The only concession she'd made to practicality was not picking a convertible from the dealership. A ragtop for the drive would have been really fun, but she knew the solid roof may prove to be handy (or important) along the way.

She'd even eschewed the automatic, wanting the chance to row through all seven gears when needed, and happily left behind ribbons of rubber and clouds of tire smoke pouring from the wheel wells when she'd left the lot after getting the quickest and cheapest deal in history on a new Corvette.

Her eyes crinkle against the sun and wind behind large, dark sunglasses. She pushes the gas pedal even deeper towards the firewall, thrilled by the howl of the quad exhaust tips releasing the spent gasses of 460 horsepower fully unleashed, and walks the car up to 130 miles per hour. There's nothing on the highway in front of her—just open road to the east of Denver and through Kansas with plenty of visibility in case there are wrecks still littering the road. Part of her isn't worried anyway; that has been a defining characteristic her whole life—just go and figure it out along the way. It'll be fine. Some people have better luck than others, some make better decisions than others, and some simply have life bounce their way all the time. Morgan is from the last grouping, knows it, and has made the most of it for three decades.

Colorado has been her home for the most of the last ten years since she was invited to leave the home she had grown up in as soon as she finished college, though she had already planned to do so anyway to gain her full freedom. The group of high school and college classmates and assorted hangers-on she'd traveled with on the western move all scattered to the wind within a couple of months after they'd arrived as they found jobs, places to stay, and new friends. Morgan hadn't cared; even though she'd hooked up with one of the boys when they still lived in New York, she quickly lost interest in him but continued to draw it out for the few weeks of the move to Colorado in order to catch the ride. Promptly dumping him within a week of arrival in Colorado, she found a house to share with some college guys from Colorado State on the northern side of Fort Collins. That was a great town, but it wasn't close enough to the larger ski resorts for her. So after the first winter, she moved southwest to Durango for a while, but then she migrated to the west of Denver into the mountains along I-70 in order to quickly get wherever she needed for whatever whim struck her.

Change is not anathema to Morgan; she's had more people flit in and out of her life than should have been possible without creating at least one lasting, meaningful relationship, but the plain truth of it is that she has but one real person who takes her as she is: her brother.

That years-ago trip was a meandering course across the country with the group stopping for gas, food, sightseeing, partying, and camping beneath the canopy of stars in the middle states' sprawling openness. It had taken several weeks. College kids with no ties to anything other than the moment.

Her departure back to New York now is going to be a fairly straight shot and, hopefully, only going to take her a pair of days if she stays clear of traffic, bad luck, and driving in the dark. No sense driving at night. She'll lock the car up tight with just the window cracked and sleep when she needs to because, even at a more reasonable rate of speed, it's too easy to come across a zombie or wreck or wild animal without enough time to stop in the depths of the much darker world she lives in. New York is going to be there, and her brother is or isn't going to be. She'll find out when she gets there. Just go and figure it out.

We do, however, need to go backward before we can move forward.

When the world came tumbling down in the fall of 2012.

***

Morgan is living in a spacious mountainside house that faces east toward Denver with a man in his midforties who is twice divorced, loaded, and—like everyone … at least, in her mind—eventually becomes a little too needy for her taste. The house is spectacular, with a sprawling wraparound porch, an outdoor, natural stone fireplace, solar panels on the roof for nearly free electrical power, and an outdoor pool and hot tub with an infinity edge so as not to interrupt the view of the peaks across the narrow valley. There's a gym in the basement, a deep well for fresh water, and massive storage rooms crammed full of food and water supplies—this man is a touch paranoid, which turns out to be a good thing … for her anyway.

The man is handsome, kind, and likes to give her gifts like a Range Rover—she'd asked for a four-door Jeep Wrangler. When he had given her a new smartphone, she demanded he take it back, and when he didn't, she managed to "lose" it repeatedly until he gave up. She can't stand and, in a way, pities those she calls "phone slaves." She's never wanted a cell and refuses to be easily found whenever. She can't abide the sight of the mobs of people living life through a tiny screen, especially out west, with its pull to be outdoors, nor can she bear the hordes of young kids clutching their phones as if they were a lifeline to something actually important other than inane stories of celebrities, nonsensical texts, and cute (stupid) photos—not a soapbox at all, *no*.

He also lavishes her with jewelry, which she neither wears nor wants—she has a serious weakness for sports equipment and keeps trying to steer him that way—and attention. It was fine for a few months with the fun, early time of any relationship, but she quickly got frustrated with his attempts to rein her in. Everyone tries that, everyone fails, and none of them learn that if you let her just be, she won't expel you from her life … or, at least, not too quickly.

Morgan doesn't use people, not by intent. It's always a two-way street, but she's typically the one who calls quits to the relationship. She can be enormously charming and generous with her attention and affection, but she's also a mystery, even to herself, as the tide changes, and she simply feels and then acknowledges it's time to move on. Many, many bruised feelings lie in her past like toppled dominoes, but she isn't someone who looks backward, ever. She lives in the moment but with an eye toward the next moment as well.

***

Those moments fall into place—suddenly and brutally—in Colorado, as they have everywhere else in the country and world. One day, Denver is a thriving and growing metropolis of well over a million people at the foothill edge of the Rockies. Less than a week later, it's a comparative ghost town littered with corpses, both animate and inanimate. For the people living farther up in the hills and those deeper into the mountains, there is a far better initial survival rate than down in town, where there are so many choices for the zombies to select from that they don't immediately bother with those outside the city.

Come right in, monsters; the buffet is now open.

All you can eat.

***

Morgan's paramour of the moment is caught down in the city when the end begins. She never hears from him; he just never comes home, which isn't particularly unusual as his business calls him out of town fairly regularly and on short notice. So at first, she isn't aware that anything is wrong. It takes her over a week after she's learned what has happened to stumble across the phone he gave her, buried in the back of a drawer, barely charged, and turned to Do Not Disturb. It's then she notices dozens of missed calls from him along with some text messages lined up in little blue bubbles.

> Hey—not going to be home on time tonight, got some extra work to do. C U later. Let's get naked.

> Are you watching TV? You need to turn the news on like now—something fuckedup is going on.

Seriously could you answer the phone or a
goddam text for once. Look at the television—
everyone is dying, we're hold up in the building
but i don't know whats going to happen because
we're surrounded by them. Call me text me
something. I need to hear form you.

Damn you Morgan—how detached from the world
can you be? Not going to be home tonight after
all or ever.

Quite a bit detached, but that's nothing new.

Like all the other cities in the country, Denver and its
suburbs screamed, suffered, and died quickly, with a good
few of those who remained standing having nothing in their
minds but the classic American dream of the pursuit of
happiness—in the form of eating their (former) fellow man.

Morgan doesn't notice anything is awry for a few days.
She isn't tuned in to the need to be connected to the grid
of constant news like so many others and is always doing
something real instead. She simply just doesn't have the
impulse to check her voice mail, her email, her texts, her
missed calls, the top twenty news stories, or what's trending.
She has no impulse to check on anything else. She's doing
what she's doing, and that's the most important thing at that
moment. None of her previous jobs required her to have a
phone, even a home one. She knows her schedule and goes
to work on time. All her social interactions with friends or

new acquaintances are simple as well—they'll meet at this place at this time. She uses actual verbal communication.

Four days AZ—"After Zombie"; Jesus isn't helping anyone anymore, thereby relinquishing control of the calendar—Morgan encounters her first zombie after her morning run up and down the nearby hills on dirt paths that wind in never-ending switchbacks and climb to the pinnacle of the nearest mini-mountain. It isn't a long distance, nothing more than three miles in each direction, but the ascent includes an altitude increase of a couple thousand feet, so it serves as her short, fast run.

As is her wont, upon returning, Morgan strips off her sweat-soaked sports top, tosses it onto one of the Adirondack chairs, and paces across the span of the deck, tugging her hair out of its ponytail and discarding the band onto a table. She takes a drink of water and settles her breathing, earbuds still in—old-school mp3 player, mind you. Removing one's top isn't a move a normal woman would do, but then again, Morgan fiercely defies most of what defines a "normal woman." She runs this route every morning, mixing a longer ten-mile run in twice a week that follows a side loop and eventually winds back to the main circuit. Her pattern after those runs in the warmer months is the same, which makes for astonishing fights at the overnight delivery companies that frequently and conveniently bring packages for her boyfriend around the same time she ends her runs. Once, one of the delivery men was welcomed at the front door by the topless woman—glistening with sweat, gorgeous, and completely indifferent to the stare—and told his coworkers about it. They literally brawl daily in the distribution center over who will be the driver of the day. She doesn't know they do this, but she does know the general reaction she causes. She really just doesn't give a shit. She's had her boobs for fifteen years, okay? They're rather nice, and there they are. The only thing she keeps an eye out for is whether the delivery men are holding a phone when they ring the doorbell—pictures are not cool. She once had to grab a guy's phone and throw it into the scrub below the house after hearing the telltale click of the fake shutter.

Music is one of the most critical pieces of Morgan's life, and she has something on at all times, whether it's while exercising, driving in the car, or playing on the golf course. She plays all different kinds of music. It helps her with the endlessly raging clutter that's in her head, which is why her favorite is complicated music—fast, busy, aggressive, and unpredictable—so she can fall in and leave the rest of the world's noise behind.

Some of her favorite bands will sneak snippets of quotes from movies or sound effects from a show or something similar, so she overlooks the first cries for help as nothing other than a layer within the current song. Then, finally, she disengages from the music enough to realize it's a real voice. She pops an earbud out, makes her way over to the railing, and looks down.

"Help! Someone, *anyone*, help me!"

It's a male voice from farther down the hill in the mixed growth that separates the houses sporadically built into the side. All of them have several acres of land and are staggered for alignment, providing complete visual privacy from the neighbors. She can't initially see who the voice is coming from, but then she sees a burst of color a hundred or so yards downhill. Something yellow flickers through an open space between trees and is followed by two more shapes of indiscriminate color. Morgan stands there and watches, trying to look ahead to the next space in order to be ready to get a clearer look of what's going on. She hears the unintelligible sounds the man is making and his labored breathing as he runs and crashes through the undergrowth. There are other sounds, too, but nothing more than a grunting or breathing of something. Is he being chased by a mountain lion? Or more than one? Really unlikely, but it's the most possible explanation. They don't usually come anywhere near a full-sized adult, but hungry is hungry sometimes.

Muuuuuuuhhhhh!

What the fuck is that?

That isn't a sound she's heard from anything, ever, and it sends a tickle of uncertainty into her stomach. Fear and Morgan aren't well acquainted, but that guttural call gives her pause. As the noises of pursuit—snapping branches, stumbling footsteps—and the evermore frantic exhalations of the pursuee close upon the house, she spins into action. Whatever it is, she can help. Besides—this jumps into her mind briefly as she crosses the deck for the Bo staff leaning against the natural stone chimney—it's been a while since she's been in a legitimate fight.

One of her fairly recent relationships was with a martial arts instructor who hadn't specialized in any one technique but rather in as many as possible in order to create flexible fighters. Learning—quickly, of course—the basics and then rapidly moving to sparring had thrilled her. Anything physical and competitive is medicine for her soul, and she immersed herself and practiced daily until she broke that boyfriend's nose and several ribs during a vigorous session. Not her fault; he'd hit her first, in the face and hard—because of jealousy, and she fell into a fugue of rage that didn't stop until he was lying on the mat at her feet, groaning. Whether his anger and jealousy were totally warranted didn't matter—there was no good reason to hit someone in a relationship. That was it for the relationship as she stalked out of the dojo, robe on and barefoot, and rode off on her bike.

Twirling the six-foot wood pole lightly in her right hand and enjoying the trickle of adrenaline seeping into her muscles, Morgan moves back to the railing and calls out, "Up here! Come around the house to the left. There are stairs!"

No direct response, but she hears the sounds of the pursuit shift direction. She moves into the middle of the dark boards and readies herself, standing with the Bo vertically in her hand, knees bent. What comes next both frees and traps Morgan.

A man in his early thirties staggers to the top of the stairs, sweat soaking his red hair and pouring down his face to saturate the yellow running shirt she glimpsed between the trees moments earlier. He's tall and thin, a typical runner's build, but he's clearly at the end of his endurance as he struggles to lift his foot onto the surface of the deck and catches a toe, stumbling down to one knee before he sees her. Rising slowly, still looking down as he does so, he speaks rapidly and with terror in his voice. "Ohmygodthankyou! We have to get inside! They're right behind me, we have to get away. Help me! They're, they're coming ...." He stops abruptly as he finally really sees her, a stunning woman without a shirt standing there in fighting position and with a bit of a grin on her face. She isn't aware she's smiling, nor does she remember that she's shirtless. "Um, you, you, what are you doing? You don't have a shirt on ... what?" he continues, completely blown away and at a standstill at the opening of the deck.

That hesitation costs him.

Muuuuuuuhhhhh!

The first zombie—though she has no clue at the time that's what it is—launches itself from the top step and lands heavily on the man's back, wrapping its arms and legs around in an abominably intimate embrace, and sinks to the now struggling runner's neck like a vampire dipping to feed or a lover reaching for the tender skin above the collarbone. The man collapses in a heap, his exhausted legs unable to support the added weight. The zombie's mouth tears away flesh as it goes down, slinging gore off in a semicircle before going back for more.

Morgan watches, stunned at first, unable to believe what she's seeing—a human attacking another human like an animal and actually *eating* him. She impulsively shouts in surprise and takes a few steps to help when a second one

achieves the top of the stairs and steps around the pile of limbs—now moving much more slowly—to face her.

Not much in life has made Morgan hold her horses, but this is one of those rarities, at least momentarily. The first one had moved quickly enough that she was unable to get a really clear look before it began feeding. This second one—this is no normal human in front of her. The gray skin stretches tightly across the bones of the skull, and there isn't anything human left in the eyes that bore into hers—not even noticing her state of deshabille—just a primal hunger and dark anger. Its clothes are torn from the run through the woods, one sneaker is missing, blood trails weakly from a deep scrape on the right side of its neck, and she doesn't want to know what that is hanging from the side of its mouth.

The monster only pauses for a second, seemingly choosing between jumping into the fray at its feet and the fresh meal in front of it, and then abruptly charges her, faster than she expected. She allows it to come close and then simply pivots to the side at the last moment, spins, and hammers the full weight of the staff into the back of its skull with a satisfying *crack* as he passes. The hit sends the creature sprawling headlong with a clatter into the chairs and tile-topped tables arranged around the stucco-colored chiminea.

She turns back toward the man now faintly moaning in pain beneath the feeding zombie and again takes a few steps, intending to help, when *that* one raises its head, blood drizzling off its chin in a dripping red ribbon that spatters the yellow shirt. It grunts as it rises and steps over the fallen body and stalks toward her. No blind charge this time, so she settles the Bo in both hands at an angle across her body, palms facing opposite directions, and strikes at the ankles. Another solid, sharp *crack* as she makes contact, and she knows she's snapped at least one bone with the blow. A human would have gone down instantly in a heap.

It doesn't fall.

No grimace of pain, no grunt, just a slight stagger from the force of the impact. It never even breaks eye contact.

Shit.

Her adrenaline level has been dragged through a roller coaster's gyrations over the last thirty minutes. It had peaked near the end of her run when her brain tried to force her body to surrender those last few ergs of energy and speed, then abated as she reached the finish line of the deck, then perked back up when she heard the first sounds of the chase, and people—and monsters—started to invade her space. Now she feels the full flood again—nostrils expanding, heart racing, eyes narrowing. She's utterly ready for this—a fight where she has to hold nothing back for the first time in her life. Morgan has been competing her entire life against everything; it's what pushes her when she's tired and keeps her going when everyone else begins to quit, and drives her just a teeny, tiny bit nuts … in a good way … mostly. In addition to her once-in-a-generation athletic prowess, she possesses the killer instinct to use it and not just to win but to dominate, demolish, and destroy her opponents. While she doesn't know it yet, the world has just presented her with what she's been seeking her entire life. As with all other things, initial success comes to her without having to think about it. Morgan wades in—any thoughts of subtlety, feints, and the balletic, sinuous beauty of the martial arts tossed aside.

This is going to be nothing other than a straight-up brawl.

The second blow lands on the monster's head, twisting its skull and spraying blood across the surface of the deck, and as she sweeps back around, the Bo hammers down on its right knee, buckling the joint so her antagonist goes down on the other knee and struggles to rapidly rise to its feet. Conscious of the other one still detangling itself from the wreckage of the furniture at the fringes of her peripheral vision—and also aware she's already exerted herself heavily today—she hurries to end this quickly. Gripping the staff at the bottom third, she swings overhead in a woodcutter's motion and, with all the force her ripped 134 pounds can muster, thunders the heavy wood into the base of the zombie's neck, the bones of the spine snapping on impact, like matchsticks exploding, severing the spinal cord in the process, and blood erupts from the stunning impact of the wound. This time, it goes down and doesn't rise, and the blood pools on the boards of the deck and drips through the gaps.

No time to admire her handiwork. She hops over the prone form and jogs the few steps toward number two. That one hears her coming and lifts its horror of a crimson-sheeted face off the surface of the deck to growl at her approach. She doesn't hesitate but drives the end of the staff into its left eye socket with a wet *thunk* and pushes her full weight into it, shoving as deeply into the skull as possible, and then lets go. The zombie goes into a spasmodic fury, clawing vainly at the six-foot protuberance, scattering furniture as its struggles speed up and then slow, then a twitch or two … and then nothing.

Blood everywhere from all three of the corpses on the deck surface, Adirondack chairs in jagged pieces, the ashes from the chiminea floating in the air and landing and twisting in the puddles of blood like sailboats for insects. The steady drizzle of the red rain hits the patio surface beneath. What a horrible mess.

Morgan stands there, chest heaving from the exertion (and excitement). Tiny rivulets of sweat mixed with blood make their way down her spectacular physique, curving into the hollows of sharply defined muscles, before continuing their journey. She marches over to the second zombie, places a muddy running shoe on its chest, and yanks the end of the Bo out with a damp popping sound. Raising it above her own head, she leans back and howls in victory, letting herself go in the cry to the clouds drifting in disinterest above. She's lived for thirty years under the rules of others. She understands instinctively—before learning far more in the next few days about what has happened—that she now gets to twist those rules any way she wants and is savagely thrilled at the prospect.

CHAPTER 2

After pacing off the adrenaline pouring through her body and beginning to hit the inevitable crash, Morgan goes into the house, pausing and then locking the French door to the deck behind her. She knows it won't stop much of anything, but she hopes, at least, for some warning if more of those things out there and they break through the glass. She also suspects they aren't terribly intelligent but simply focus on attacking like the ones on the deck did, so they could just be stopped by something as simple as a lock. She has no clue where the annoying cell phone is, so she goes to the house phone, lifts the handset, dials her boyfriend Malcolm's mobile number, and hits Talk. Nothing. The power is on, the number keys are all lit, but there's no sound at all. She tries his office number, thereby exhausting two of the three numbers she has committed to memory, with the same result. In disgust, she drops the phone with a clatter onto the caramel-colored marble countertop, leaves the kitchen, and moves deeper into the sprawling home. She searches briefly for her cell phone without luck and tries the other phones in the house to no effect. Flipping on the television mounted over the stacked stone fireplace is no better—while the power clicks to life, the screen only shows a No Signal message.

Okay. Phone lines are down, cable is out, two something or others just killed a guy on my deck, and I killed both of them, she thinks as a small measure of unease creeps into her consciousness. Despite her disdain for most of the people on the planet and the way things have been trending, the idea that there are monsters on the loose killing people causes her to shiver. The only technological pleasure she allows herself is horror movies—the scarier and messier, the better. She just loves the thrill of sitting under a blanket in the dark and waiting for something to jump out and maul the idiot characters into bits and pieces. *Living* in a horror story is another story.

Zombies? Could those things have been actual zombies?

Wouldn't that be something. The world at large was fascinated by them in the recent past, with television shows, movies, and books about the dead-but-living proliferating like Gremlins in a swimming pool.

Going inside the house, she sheds what's left of her exercise clothes, showers—albeit a tad nervously and, as a result, rather quickly—and then dresses in a long-sleeved cotton shirt, pants, and more durable shoes and ties her hair tightly into a low ponytail that drapes down her back. Her plan is to scout the surrounding area's houses to see if she can find anyone who knows what has happened and, if not, hunt for a gun or two. Though sparsely populated across the immediate surroundings, there are a dozen homes within a half-mile radius. She spends the rest of the discovery day preparing and gathering. Something instinctive tells her that the two whatevers she just dispatched are not the only ones around. Malcolm has not returned home, it is almost too quiet in the area, and now that she thinks back to her run, there was literally no one out on the trail, which is uncommon. Plus, the man being chased had obviously been pursued for quite a long distance and time.

Her boyfriend isn't a gun person. "Guns kill people, baby," he'd say. Really? Guns just jump out of a drawer by magic and shoot people at random? She disagreed with him strongly on the topic but never bothered to draw the fight out since she never cared one way or the other about owning a gun. She just liked to argue (foolish) topics like that one for fun when her opposition felt very strongly about them. There are no firearms in his house, but she has her Bo and a wickedly sharp machete from the pile of gardening tools in the garage. No one actually uses machetes at home; lots of people buy them, maybe because they're as close to a sword as people who don't work at a Renaissance Festival can get … or maybe men are just dorks. This one, however, is going to be put to use, and she figures out how to strap it along her right thigh. She's not too worried though. She's confident she will be able to acquire firearms somewhere. Beating the shit out of those creatures has been spectacular exercise and deeply thrilling for her on a primal level, but she knows it's risky to go hand-to-hand with anything, especially if there are larger groups.

She doesn't relish touching any of the bodies littering the deck, but she likes the thought of leaving them there a lot less. Locating a heavyweight canvas tarp in the garage, she lays it out next to each of the corpses in turn and uses the Bo as a lever to flip them onto the fabric. The whatevers are first. Once they are on the cloth, she drags them around the front of the house, down the driveway, and across the street, breathing heavily from the effort. A fairly shallow but steep, dry gully feeds under the road into a galvanized ribbed culvert, and that becomes their final resting place as she tips them out of the tarp. She makes the mistake of watching the first one flop heavily down the slope, arms and legs tumbling in sickening, unnatural ways, until coming to a rest at the bottom. It stares back uphill in her direction with accusing eyes that she knows see nothing, but it unsettles her nonetheless. The second whatever is deposited without any fanfare. She yanks the tarp up until she feels the body slip off, and then she goes back to the house right away.

The normal guy lets out a gassy sigh as she turns him over, and for a moment, she thinks he's still alive. But a closer look at the damage done to his neck proves this isn't possible. Parts of his spine are visible through the ragged hole torn in the flesh, and she quickly turns her eyes away, flicking the base of the Bo under a corner of the bone-colored cloth and covering his face. Her preference is not to put him in the same spot as the other bodies, at first feeling like it's inappropriate to mix them up, but then she decides dead is dead and none of them are going to be upset. Not wanting to watch his awkward traverse downhill, she repeats the same process as with the last whatever and then wads up the tarp and, without looking closely, throws it in with the bodies.

Uphill or downhill?

It probably doesn't matter, but she decides that deeper into the road and farther away from civilization improves her odds of finding someone else, so she sets off uphill along the edge of the dusty asphalt. What she doesn't know right away is that it *has* been four days already ....

Like Morgan, the house is almost entirely off the grid. Power is supplied by the solar panels to keep the lights on and run the electricity for everything down to the pump for the well, which moves water through the house. She's literally gone through the first few days after the world ended without a clue that anything is amiss.

***

Several hours later, Morgan trudges back to the house annoyed—which is a smidge of her natural state anyway—tired, dusty, and confused. And better armed. She's visited every house within striking distance and has no more answers than when she left; nothing but questions hang in the cooling afternoon air. No one was in any of the eight homes she went through, though, in several, there were signs of a hasty exit: partially eaten meals littered deserted plates, dresser drawers hung open like loose teeth, and most exterior doors had been left ajar.

After going through three or four houses, finding nobody, and moving on, she began searching the remaining homes more carefully for guns and survivors. Naturally, she found none of the latter, and after an initially frustrating discovery of several locked gun cabinets in the house of an obvious hunter (at which time a mountain lion startled her momentarily, staring at her from a shadowy corner, and she almost reversed course and hauled ass out of the house before realizing three things: she wasn't going to be faster than it anyway, she was still looking for something of a fight, and after a dozen eternal seconds drifted past, she was able to see that the damn thing was just stuffed), she finally found a shotgun and what she thought might be a Glock, though she wasn't an expert. There was some ammunition as well, and she eventually headed back home as fully armed as one could be for the time being.

***

After eating some salad with leftover grilled chicken for dinner and drinking more water, she scouts the house to confirm all the doors and windows are closed and locked. Malcolm has an office upstairs in a Victorian-style turret that juts into the sky from a corner of the master bedroom via a spiral staircase that leads to a trapdoor, of all things. When he first showed her the office, she laughed at him, but now she's glad for it. It isn't a huge room, perhaps fifteen feet in diameter, but the floor-to-ceiling windows around its entire circumference provide an incredible panoramic vista that reveals the wilderness surrounding the house, making a visitor feel as if they're literally sitting atop the world. There's a computer on the desk, a half bath, and a couch, but otherwise, the space is empty and simple. Morgan slides the desk on top of the trapdoor with some effort, piles her weapons on the floor within arm's reach near the couch, and then turns off the desk lamp. For a few moments, she stands at the windows facing Denver and lets her eyes adjust to see what she can see.

What she sees is nothing.

Deep black darkness stretches out before her without a single glimmer of light or life. Without realizing it, she looks in each direction, hopefully seeking some sign of life. There's none, just endless depths of ebony, like the center of the heart of Satan.

Sleep is a long time coming.

***

Morgan awakens with the sunrise erupting into a cloudless sky the following morning, and it takes a minute or two for reality to reassert itself. She's alone in the house (not a problem). She has light and heat, which is good since winter is looming sooner than she knows. There are three corpses across the street (not so good), and she has no clue what the hell is going on (rather annoying).

After a light breakfast of just eggs, she gets herself dressed and armed and leaves the house in the Range Rover to head down the hill. It's a short drive—there isn't a single car moving on I-70 heading east toward Denver, though there are a fair number of inert vehicles on the sides of the road and an occasional one to avoid in the driving lanes. No people are in sight either; it's just as silent in the outskirts of the city. Silent and unmoving, which should have been impossible given the size of the population.

It isn't until she reaches the city itself, coming off the interstate as it drops into downtown, that she comes across signs of life. Well ... whatever life passes for now. Packs of the creatures she encountered yesterday rove fairly aimlessly and shuffle through the streets. Several of them swing around at the sound and sight of her SUV and begin to pursue in a lurching stumble, but she quickly leaves them behind in her rearview mirror as she winds her way toward Malcolm's office building. The farther she drives through the cool concrete and glass canyons of the city, the more of them there are, and she's glad for the solid vehicle around her, as their numbers quickly become unsettling. She can see nearly one hundred of them scattered around the sidewalks and roads like drunken, mobile chess pieces of all shapes and sizes.

Crossing a few streets until she reaches the area near the baseball park, she scans everything in her line of sight. Seeing nothing, she parks in front of a nearby brewpub. After sliding the shotgun off the passenger seat and setting the machete into its holster on her thigh, she locks the door and stands in front of the aged-brick façade of the building. Many of the buildings in this section of the city are rehabs, but enough were left untouched during the restoration work to retain some character.

Malcolm's office is on an upper floor, and she knows she'll have to take the stairs to reach it—there are no lights on anywhere in the city even though some were probably left on when everyone fled; she finally realizes she has power due to the solar panels on the house.

As she enters the lobby area and scans it (nothing), she locates the entry to the stairs off to the right behind a clay planter holding a palm tree whose branches reach toward the skylights three stories above their fronds. Morgan removes the machete from its holster with a quiet *shring*. If she needs to defend herself, the Bo will be too wide for the stairwell. Being such a dedicated fan of horror movies, she has the inherent fear that this is where she'll be attacked, and her otherwise unshakable confidence slips a bit. Glancing back through the glass doors that lead to the street, she sees a couple of creatures wander past, and that really pushes her to act. She marches across the lobby, sets the Bo down in the corner, and pulls the brass handle to the stairway door, jumping backward as she does so. Nothing leaps out at her, but as she glimpses inside, she feels a tremor of anxiety again.

Pitch. Fucking. Black.

Of course it is; it's an inside stairway, the lights are out, and she has no other way to go up. Luck—the good kind, anyway—is hard to come by in the new world, though she's only beginning to learn that lesson. There isn't a reception desk in the lobby, so there's no chance of finding a flashlight, and the door is hinged to close by itself; the only thing in the lobby she could use to prop it open is the planter holding the palm tree, and that has to weigh at least five hundred pounds. She tries to see if the door will open wide enough to allow the Bo to wedge into the corner of the frame, but it's a no go, so she leaves it resting on the floor between the door and frame. There's a sliver of light a couple of inches wide that dies to less than a birthday candle's glow a few feet into the open space of the steel stairs leading up toward Malcolm's offices on the third floor. Morgan steps through, eases the door against the Bo as quietly as she can, and then just stands still, waiting for her eyes to adjust and listening for any sound. From what little she's seen and experienced so far, they aren't exactly subtle creatures, but she can't be sure whether or not there are any sneaky ones, so she holds her spot for two, then three minutes, breathing steadily through her nose.

No sounds.

She's able to see the base of the first few steps in the slender finger of light, so she edges closer, raises the machete, and begins to creep up the stairs, putting her weight on the balls of her feet and pausing every couple of steps to listen again. Ascending to the first small landing that turns 180 degrees, she glances up, hoping, to no avail, that a door farther up is open and throwing some light into the space. The second half of the first level goes more quickly, but as she reaches the second floor's landing, her heart is pounding heavily for someone as fit as she is, and sweat is slithering down her back. There are three doors, all closed, on her left. More waiting, more listening, more nothing. She darts past the closed doors and goes as rapidly up the next level as she can in the dark and then pauses outside the door to Malcolm's office space. She has no idea if he's going to be here or if he's been traveling. *Will he be dead inside, or worse, will he be like one of those things?* Part of her just wants to turn around, go back to the car, and head home to decide what to do next. This feeling shocks her. She's usually the one who jumps in first and figures everything out second without any advance thought to the consequences, and so far that has (mostly) worked out well over the years. There was that one time during spring break in Cancun where parasailing went a little sideways, but none of the injuries were permanent other than a few scars as souvenirs of a fun week.

Recognizing her hesitation as fear, her anger rises, and in typical Morgan fashion, she forcefully expels the concept from her mind, grits her teeth, takes a few deep breaths to steady her breathing and heart rate, and moves onward to open the frosted-glass door of the office space. Malcolm isn't any more significant to her than any of his predecessors, but she decides she wants to know what has happened and help him if he's trapped or injured or hiding. She also wants to prove to herself that fear is just another obstacle to be seen, analyzed, and discarded since she's ultimately the only audience she cares about.

Finally some light. Floor-to-ceiling windows face the street, and she's thankful for the illumination after the inky dark of the stairs. Sunlight comes in strong rays to light nothing more remarkable than the dust motes drifting aimlessly in the warmth. She waits again, scanning the low cubes that occupy most of the floor and listening for any sounds. There's an out-of-date, dark green shag carpet on the floor that Malcolm insisted on for noise reduction and walking comfort, which she's now glad for since it will allow her to move without a sound.

Now more confident, she can feel the sweat drying stickily on her back as her heart rate settles to its ordinary pace. There's an odor in the air she doesn't much care for. She has an idea what it is, so she moves cautiously through the cube farm toward the closed door of Malcolm's office. Any chance he's holed up in there with the door locked? She thinks it unlikely but silently pads forward to the door. Trying the burnished nickel handle, she finds it unlocked and levers it down; she eases the door open and is startled by a noisome *crrreeeeeak*. *Dammit*, she thinks, though she's more aggravated by her twitchy reaction than by the sound itself. There's no one in the office, so she resigns herself to the idea that he's likely dead. She turns to go to the Range Rover but stops in her tracks.

A woman, backlit by the strong sunshine that comes through the windows and makes her face invisible, stands between her and the exit door. Long dark hair cascades over her shoulders. Morgan takes a quick step forward, raising her non-machete hand in greeting, figuring this must be one of Malcolm's staff who was hiding until the noise from the door brought her out. She's completely right.

Muuuuuuuhhhhh!

It charges immediately, hair flying out behind it in contrails, like a swarm of yellow jackets disturbed into fury by an invader. Had Morgan not run into the two creatures on her deck, she would have been dead before she had time to scream. Where anyone uninitiated would have paused in shock, her training and instinct take over, and she drops to a knee to avoid the groping arms as the monster races at her,

and then she swings the machete in a flat arc behind her as it passes. There's a brief resistance of flesh and bone, but the blade is ravenously sharp, and she swung with malice.

Thump.

Morgan rises into a battle-ready stance immediately, not looking at the arm that's lying on the deep carpet, blood spewing and staining the green to black. For its part, the creature seems no more bothered by losing the limb than a person would be by a mosquito bite. It briefly glances down at the guttering spray of blood being propelled out of the stump, then raises its eyes and fixes its gaze on her and charges again. This time, Morgan doesn't duck but sidesteps to the armless side and repeats the backward swing with all her strength.

A louder *thump*, followed by another even louder one just a moment later, and then silence.

Among the many possible definitions of the word "freedom," perhaps two are the most powerful: the complete surrender to and immersion in lust, and the freedom to kill.

Morgan has now experienced both and is finding that with practice, she rather likes the latter.

She walks down the stairs, gets in her car, and drives away, leaving another short chapter of her life in the rearview mirror—a truncation, as always, but messier. Thunder chuckles happily in the distance, echoing in a smooth grumble against the rising slopes of the Rockies as she drives back toward the house and sanctuary. The gathering clouds look less welcoming, sprawling to the far northwestern horizon in mammoth thunderheads, brief flickers of lightning strobing in their depths.

***

Morgan has been in Colorado for close to ten years now, migrating around the state as her whims or the winds take her. A year in Fort Collins, some down in Durango, and the last few in the Denver area, though never too close to the city since people generally annoy her. As she moves around, she makes just a single concession to the growing wave of being in touch with everything all the time: an email account so she can stay in touch with her brother. There's no point in sending him her mailing address as that tends to change annually, if not sooner, but he had insisted she get the email account until she finally agreed. Other than that, she is as about off the grid as a person can be in this century. Even though she eventually got a phone from Malcolm, she hasn't shared the number since she can't be relied upon to have the damn gadget with her. She doesn't own a computer either—she goes to the library weekly and checks in with her brother from one of the kiosks there. No contact with her parents, high school or college friends, or former coworkers or lovers. Unlike her brother, who holds memories of his past close to his heart (perhaps too close), visiting them from time to time like a favorite book he loves to reread, she always looks forward. There are some fond recollections of their times at the upstate New York cabins and surrounding area, that's true, but otherwise, when something is over for Morgan, it's over.

***

In the past, there was always employment available for an uncomfortably attractive woman who also happened to be an elite athlete. Her jobs, while never terribly lucrative or long-lasting—she could care less about money beyond its facility as a tool to acquire the very few things she really needs, but she still manages to accumulate a good bit of it due to her ascetic lifestyle and men's insistence on supporting her—have been as varied as her addresses. The only thing most of them have in common is that they had been outdoors. Some of them had ended spectacularly; with others, she had simply informed her manager that she was done and walked out on the spot without a care for unpaid wages or benefits or anything else.

Ski instructor, one of her favorite jobs due to the free access it had given her to the increasingly expensive resorts, had occupied each of her winters. Every day was a slog through the locals, who were trying to become better skiers without releasing their fear or working hard at it, or the visiting tourists, who came west to find that the mountains out there dwarfed most of the East Coast ones and wanted a brushup before going out, or the horrid families with small children drizzling snot across their faces as their mothers insisted they were good athletes and the fathers tried not to get caught ogling Morgan's obviously statuesque figure beneath her snug winter attire. But at the end of every shift, Morgan got to go off by herself to the most secluded, dangerous sections of the mountain and test herself. It was even better if it was snowing heavily enough to occlude everything outside of fifty yards so she could pretend she was alone in the world. The solitude and purity of days like *that* soothed her after days like *this*:

Tourist Mother: "I don't understand. You've been teaching little Billy here for two hours, and he's still snowplowing instead of parallel skiing! I thought you were supposed to be a good instructor. The Andersons recommended you highly!"

Morgan, trying really, *really* hard to be polite (really) since she had a good idea how this was going to go: "Well, you said he's five years old and that he's never skied before. What exactly were you expecting to happen?"

Tourist Mother, with condescension drizzling from every word: "Dear, we've got guests coming out from the Hamptons, you know, on 'The Island' [yes, she used air quotes] to visit us, and we're going to go with them up to Breckenrange or something like that, and their son Winthrop Northwood III apparently can ski on the moguls already as he's been taking lessons since he was three years old. We simply can't have Billy falling behind! It will hurt his feelings and could impact his development as a person. His confidence can be shattered at this tender age! You obviously wouldn't understand that since you obviously don't have children."

Billy just looked back and forth between the two women during the whole exchange, his orange-helmeted head swiveling like a tennis spectator at midcourt. His overweight father, stuffed (barely) into his own skiing gear and looking miserable—probably needed to take a leak and escape from his wife—had found an ideal vantage point to the side of the women, nodding his head at the right time behind his mirrored goggles, but Morgan knew he was really just admiring her outstanding profile, especially when compared to the ever-raging turnip the woman he'd married had turned into.

Morgan: "I see. So you want your five-year-old kid to feel like he's competing with everyone else, even at this early age, instead of just having fun and being outdoors, and, you know, being a *kid*. You're one of *those* parents. Okay, I get it. Were you expecting a participation trophy, too, at the end of the lesson?"

"*Excuse* me?" Came the shrill response, delivered with the righteous outrage that had always gotten its way in the past. "You can't speak to me that way! You work here. We're *paying* you! I need to speak to your manager. *Now!*" She rotated her head in every direction, demanding the attention to her outburst from onlookers—who all looked away, nothing to see here folks, though a few surreptitiously whipped out their phones to capture the moment—and seeking someone more important to batter next.

"Actually, I *can* speak to you that way," Morgan replied calmly, reaching to the zipper of her jacket, twisting her photo ID off, and tossing it into the snow near the woman's completely impractical and wildly expensive boots. "Seems to me like more people ought to speak to you that way, like your husband over there, who's hiding behind his goggles and hoping you'll just stay pissed at me and not take it out on him next. Does it feel good to be angry all the time?"

Morgan turned her gaze to the husband, who was cringing at this point. She'd tried not to lose it, but somewhere between "pissed" and "next," she decided she had to say what she was thinking. This tended to happen a lot and typically turned out the same way: her finding a new job. But that was easy; there were lots of ski resorts and golf courses in Colorado. She simply couldn't stand the way people had increased the shitty factor in how they acted toward one another. What happened when all of them had new BMWs, big houses, big boobs, and big paychecks and couldn't figure out their own hierarchy? Not that she knew it at the time, of course, but in the not-too-distant future, this problem was going to take care of itself in a messy hurry. "Hey, buddy, have you gotten a good enough eyeful for some mental material when you're in the bathroom alone later? Yes, I've seen you staring for the last two hours. Need me to unzip the top a little bit?"

Both of the adults were speechless. The man's jaw literally hanging agape as he contemplated the horror of the rest of the day and vacation. The woman's mouth opened, then closed, then opened again like a fish. Not a peep. That was probably a first for her.

Morgan crouched down in front of Billy, who had no idea what had just happened except that his Mom was now mad, though he was already used to that. "Hey, kid, I'm sorry this is how you're growing up. You probably don't understand this, but here is what you need to do: have fun, be a kid, run around, and don't worry about what everyone else thinks.

Sorry, too, for talking back to your mom, but I get angry when people get stupid. Don't talk back to grownups."

Billy nodded his head at the nice lady who'd told him he was doing great and was going to be fine, things he never heard from his parents. Of course, there's no way he fully understood what was going on. He was hoping for another piece of chocolate, which had been his prize for executing good turns or coming to a stop without falling face-first in the snow.

"Did you have fun today?" Morgan asked the clueless child.

His eyes darted back and forth between her and his stewing mother—who both cared for him and terrified him at times—but finally answered in a small voice, "Uh huh … I mean, yes, ma'am."

"Good. Do you like skiing?"

He nodded. "Yes, ma'am."

"Okay, even better. You keep going the way I taught you and don't worry about moguls or Windbag Northwind the XXIII or whatever his name is. You just have a good time."

Billy nodded for a final time, though was disappointed—he didn't receive another chocolate, which, truth be told, he could afford to skip—and turned to pepper his father with questions about skiing. His father was thrilled for the distraction for a change and turned away from the confrontation to attend to his son.

Morgan stood back up and faced the woman, pointing at her ID tag lying in the snow. "Hey, when you find someone else to bitch at, since I know you're going to, do me a favor and give that tag to them and tell them I'm all done." She marched off to gather her skis and head up the hill for a last run, but then she paused after a few steps and turned back. One more shot—she just couldn't help it. "Oh, and have a *really* nice afternoon."

Another unintelligible screech, which, happily, was swept away by the cold Colorado breeze, taking the ugly words off into the distance of the snowcapped mountains that stretched to the horizon. Without any success—or much honest effort—Morgan tried to suppress the wicked grin lighting up her lovely features as she sauntered away, ensuring that the shake in her hips was obvious.

"Say something!" she heard the screeching voice say. "Do something! She can't talk to me like that! Wait, you were going to jerk off thinking about her? How did she know that? Tell me! That's disgusting! You think *she's* attractive? You do, don't you? What is *wrong* with you?"

***

Golf courses used to provide her warm-weather employment. Usually as a teaching pro, but she also could be found using the cart to run beer out to the players, bartending back at the clubhouse, or washing carts at the end of the day. Like with skiing, she was content to suffer through the day's indignities—*Hey, sweetie, gimme a Bud Light. Here's a five-dollar tip. Why don't you find me at the end of my round, and I'll buy you a beer? What are you doing later?*—to reach the end of the work shift and go out on the course alone and without a cart. No sounds other than her ball striking, no thoughts other than how to craft the next shot and the one following it. She had to, as always, decline repeated offers of company when she went out; she wasn't interested in small talk, driving contests (which she'd win against all but the very, *very* best male golfers), someone staring at her figure as she twisted through the flattering contortions required for a good swing, or any of that.

Golf is another balm for the ever-present swarm of her thoughts, and the laser focus she can impose on any sport helps her settle the cloud of distraction for a few hours at least. It's during any individual physical contest that her temper vanishes; leaving only her and whatever ball is in front of her or whichever challenge of sweat beckons to be conquered. That's all Morgan understands.

The topography out west made for fascinating golfing layouts: either dead flat other than whatever artificial variation the designers had imposed on the end of the mid-American plains, or wild ascensions, declines, and sidehill misery carved into the face of the rocky soil. One tee box will grant you the privilege of being a driving hero, looking down at the green sprawl of a fairway, inviting even a modest golfer the chance to find his—or her, in Morgan's case—ball three hundred or more yards away from where they currently stood. The next can bring a ninety-yard par three with nothing more complicated (sarcasm vehemently intended) than an uphill shot over a boulder the size of a mobile home standing on end with an arrow painted on its face that told you where the flag was hidden. Anything was possible, which kept up Morgan's interest in the game over the years, depending on where she'd lived, and kept her handicap right around scratch. From the blue tees.

However, her employment at golf courses was usually transitory as well. Eventually, she would rub someone the wrong way with her blunt—some might say "tactless"— honesty or standoffishness.

As a teaching pro, she had also preferred to work with kids because they didn't ogle her figure all the time and were blank slates that didn't need bad habits broken before good ones could be developed. However, golf lessons were expensive, and most of her clients had preferred to spend their spare money on lessons for themselves.

She also preferred female clients because they largely ignored the macho bullshit that got in the way of most men becoming good golfers. Straight down the middle, clean contact, refined touch around and on the greens. These were what most women were seeking aside from the few teenage girls intent on driving the ball as far as the young pros on television. Women also largely accepted the fact that Morgan was stronger and better than they were. Therefore, they limited their competition to that of themselves versus the course itself without being concerned about who'd mashed their drive the farthest.

Men, on the other hand, mostly went about golf the wrong way. Teenage boys only wanted maximum distance off the tee and were prepared to take the risk of an aggressive swing, pounding the ball out of bounds from time to time in order to satisfy their ego with an infrequent clean stroke down the center of the fairway. Morgan had little patience for them, and of course, they spent a great deal of time eyeballing her and winking, smirking, and nudging one another during group lessons, thinking she didn't notice. When this occurred, she happily instructed them to:

"Swing hard, that's right."

"Make sure you grip the club *really* firmly."

"Yes, you should definitely look up to see how far the ball is going as soon as you possibly can. You don't want to lose sight of it, do you?"

"No, you should never take the conservative play and get your ball safely back out into the fairway when you're in the woods. If you have even the smallest of windows between two or more trees and can try to hit the ball with a full swing, you totally should. That's what the pros do, right?"

The little morons would soak it up, swing practically out of their shoes, occasionally hitting one a good distance, and run around high-fiving their buddies. She would spend her real attention on those who wanted to actually learn, breaking down the complicated parts of the game into pieces they could understand and practice. While, for the most part, she wasn't interested in other people's wins or losses, she couldn't help but feel fulfilled when one of her younger students would hit a ball just right and turn to her with the genuinely happy and innocent smile only a child could create.

Adult men were another problem. They almost all *had* to measure themselves by their distance off the tee, many of them playing a set of tees farther back than they should simply so they could say they did. Just about every lesson began with a conversation of what they wanted to accomplish, and aside from the juvenile flicker of eyes roaming up and down her figure, they nearly all wanted to add length—which brought its own juvenile snicker to her mind. She always had a stable of loyal customers, though she didn't fool herself into thinking at least half of that loyalty was due to her looks, but money was green regardless why it was handed over. She was pretty numb to the nonsense anyway. Morgan always made an effort to work on the parts of their game that were actually flawed—putting, iron accuracy, and so on—but given a choice, they were content to stand stubbornly at the range, trying over and over to just hit the ball farther. They listened more closely than the teenage boys, and she saw them making the adjustments she'd suggested, but she also watched them inevitably turn to how far they could hit the ball as their true measuring stick.

Out of everything she taught, her favorite way to teach involved lessons on the course, where she and the client would go out and work on situational golf, often hitting three or four balls from the same spot with different clubs, stances, and swings. She would bring her own clubs with her, but she rarely hit a ball, usually just grabbing one to illustrate the swing path or make a visual point. Impatient clients would just want to play the round together without putting the actual work in. She preferred not to teach that way since it instantly became a competition between her and the customer, and she was going to win in every phase of the game, especially the mental part. If the customer hit a nice tee shot that was beyond her range to match, she'd simply play a 3-wood instead of driver off the tee, silently conceding the distance and letting him "win" but also making it obvious that she was choosing not to hit driver and thereby weakening his victory. She would then, however, work her way down the hole in spectacular fashion while focusing only on the terrain and how to win against the course. Inevitably, he would make an error, and at the end of the hole, she'd have typically scored no worse than par while her customer would be scratching his head at how he outdrove an actual golf pro but still ended up with double bogey.

"I don't get it. I've been paying all this money and still don't score much better than I did when I first started lessons with you." This was a pretty typical conversation and always came with an underlying hint of accusation.

"Well, have you ever just thought about whether you're a better golfer overall, not focusing on the score but on whether you make fewer mistakes, hit the ball more cleanly, or have much shorter putts for par?" They'd always gotten better, but their improvement didn't always show up as a steady downward progress on scores. If everyone got a stroke or two better per round, they'd all be on TV. Golf was miserable work for modest reward.

The clients would usually think a moment or two before replying, clearly noticing that she was actually right, but still stubbornly cling to the number on the card as proof. "Yes, but I'm still stuck right around the midnineties and just can't seem to get over that hump into the eighties."

"Have you been going to the range like I told you, spending a day only on a single club and learning how to hit that one consistently? Not hitting a dozen five-irons and then banging away at the driver?"

Every single time, their eyes would duck left before answering, instantly telling her the truth for both the missed range time and which club had been used. "Of course I have. I have to tell you, Morgan, that I'm frustrated. I feel like our arrangement is completely one way, with me spending all the money and all of the time and getting nothing in return."

Ah, here we go.

This was an ancient conversation in the world of man and woman. She was an expert at keeping it a short one since she'd had more than enough practice. She also enjoyed having the conversation in her outdoor voice so there would be witnesses. "Oh, I see. So this isn't about golf. It's about you exchanging money for *my* time—which I'm spending too—not listening to my instructions, and feeling like your money entitles you to a glance down my top or up my shorts. Yes, buddy, they're called 'boobs' and 'ass,' and all women have them. The job title, though, is Golf Pro not Golf Ho.

The only round thing you're supposed to be looking at, in case you missed that, is the tiny, white ball down there on the ground. Lesson one, remember? Keep your eye on the *ball*. Not the boob."

Cue spluttering indignation, red face, spots of sweat on the brow as the men cast their eyes around to see who was listening, and then a demand to speak to the manager. Yup, pretty much how it would go, and so she'd stroll off the course and try to locate the man's wife on her way out and whisper something sweet like, "Your husband is *so* big and rich, and you are *such* a lucky woman." Shrieks to follow … .

***

It's never as simple as winning for her. Domination of the event and opponent is required; grinding them into mental and physical surrender by the end is her goal. This didn't go over all that well (for everyone else) when she played youth sports. Even at the tender age of seven or eight, she would continue to press the score and play at full speed, heedless of the bruised feelings elsewhere on the field, reveling in the absolute acquiescence of her opponents. Her competitiveness carried into her teenage, young adult, and full adulthood psyche. Glory before grace. Too many were the occasions where her parents had to physically drag or carry her away, howling in frustrated, impotent, and tearful rage, at the end of a game her team had lost. It wasn't so much because they lost the game but rather how they played. If her teammates had given something less than what she had expected of them—their absolute best—the cries on the way to the car were outrageous compared to those heard in these kinder days of everyone getting a trophy for showing up. After about the age of ten, her parents flipped a coin for who got to skip the match and avoid the embarrassment of having that kid who was not only much better than her peers on the field but also a competitive monster. Her brother, however, never skipped an opportunity to watch Morgan impose herself on an athletic contest, and while a fierce competitor (and notable athlete) in his own right, he didn't have the same ruthless killer instinct on the playing field.

For all the misery she delivered to little kids back in the day and to grownups more recently, her ferocious nature will definitely serve her well during these days after the end of the world.

CHAPTER 3

Like most of the survivors of what those who read the Bible call the "Apocalypse and Resurrection" (though those who do read it have some trouble wrapping their heads around what has happened and whether they can spin it into a benign sign from God), Morgan has become a gatherer; she accumulates supplies such as food, water, and weapons of any kind, including guns and ammo, from the surrounding houses and stores. Locating a nearby ranchers' supply outlet, she brings back thousands of yards of razor wire and over the span of several days, strings it carefully through tree branches up to a height of six feet around the loose perimeter of her property. Worried about elk or other creatures stumbling into it, she also hangs from the wire dozens of miniature sleigh bells she found at a craft store, knowing the animals will avoid them, but the zombies likely won't pick up the alert. Standing on the deck and looking over her work one dusky evening, she has the thought that all she needs are some Christmas decorations and blinking lights and she'll be all set.

The wire does its job, keeping her own compound a safe haven, and from time to time, she'll go out in the morning to discover a zombie wound up tightly in the gleaming strands, bleeding from dozens of wounds as it struggles to free itself but managing only to become more deeply enmeshed in the shredding barbs. The deep gashes inflicted go unnoticed by the mockery of a human who only thinks of killing and eating. Once or twice, Morgan simply stands there and watches for a few moments, studying the actual horror show most of mankind has become, noticing that as soon as they sense her, they become abruptly still and wait, as if trying to be invisible, and then lunge wildly for her once she's within a few feet, only to be savaged further by the restraining ribbons of metal. Eventually, she loses interest and fires a single pistol shot into the forehead, hearing the report echo multiple times down the hillside until fading into the stillness of a world ending.

She's also become a hunter, taking almost daily forays out into the nearby streets to eliminate any of the close-in monsters and secure her immediate area—or at least scour it clean of the scourge that has quickly become the new majority. The Range Rover is now parked and collecting dust in the driveway in favor of a dark green, four-door Jeep Wrangler she's always wanted. Both vehicles are equally capable ones for on- and off-road duty; it's a matter of the Jeep feeling more like "her," and she prefers its knobby tires over the highway tires on the luxury SUV and the outlandish array of extra lights on the Jeep that flood the area ahead in stunning clarity.

In the first days of patrolling, she went on foot, hiking in patterns around her house to visit others, taking inventory of which ones held supplies she needed to come back for, and closing those houses back up so that when she returned for water, guns, blankets, and more, she wouldn't have any surprises. As the range of her cleared areas expands, she takes the Jeep through the rudimentary gate she fashioned across the span of the driveway and farther down the hill to particular stores. Once she'd accumulated enough food and extra water and other matériel, however, she got bored and initiated hunting trips where the only purpose was to whittle down the population of zombies littering the streets of Denver and the encircling suburbs.

Those trips escalate as time passes. Always comfortable with silence and her own company for long stretches, after a handful of months pass, Morgan only barely registers subconsciously that she's teetering beyond where it's okay to be on her own. Without company or a job to maintain routines and contact with (living) people, and having ended the pattern of scouting and collecting, she has started to descend a bit into the never-ending depths of madness. This happens to many of the survivors who find themselves isolated after a lifetime of people everywhere all the time. It has happened to her brother, though she doesn't know he still lives or that his foray onto the golf course is what swings the pendulum back to sane. It's early yet, and oddly, what keeps her on the right side of her mind is the zombie population.

Normal people need a destination or distraction when they're on vacation to give them something to do, especially those without a family. Singles will find themselves rattling around their house or apartment or wherever they live, fighting paralysis by analysis or drifting and playing hours of solitaire on their computer while thinking about nothing, and then, suddenly, the week is gone. Morgan is unlike this, incapable of being still or unoccupied, and she loathes "distraction by gadget"—medical term coming soon to a fat kid near you—and is drawn to the outdoors whenever possible. Many have been the days when she happily went for a run in thick spring thunderstorms that boomed across the usually dry hillsides spotted by aspens and evergreens. She'd return saturated through every stitch of every garment she wore. Golf in the rain hadn't bothered her either, and of course, skiing in weather that most would have called miserable was always a beckoning challenge to her.

Those compulsive competitive instincts drive her to increase the distance from sanctuary, simplify the weapons she carries, and heighten the risk in all the situations. It's a test, over and over, to prove to herself she can do it, can win, can stand above them all. That this newest game has a mortal outcome doesn't matter and, in fact, thrills her at a primal level. It nudges her ever closer to less sane, too, but as long as there are opponents, she's going to be okay, whether she knows it or not.

At first, she would go out, fully armed with a sawed-off shotgun dangling between her shoulder blades in a holster that wraps around her torso and crosses between her breasts on a worn leather strap with slots to hold spare magazines for the handguns and shells for the shotgun, the machete strapped to her right thigh, a pistol at each hip, and the ever-present Bo. She'd wish she had a dog to keep her company and for early warnings, but she'd make do by silently tracking smaller packs of zombies and eliminating them with the pistols from a distance, the shotgun as they inevitably charge headlong and out of control to get closer, and then the Bo or machete for the one or two that get in close enough for hand-to-hand elimination.

"Pssst," she'd whisper at a small pack doing the zombie shuffle down a Denver street.

Nightmare faces would swivel around at the sound, make eye contact, and howl.

Muuuuuuuhhhhh!

After a few of those, she'd wish they have something else to say, so to speak.

What comes next is their mad dash to what they see as an easy meal, but it would turn out as anything but.

Within a short period of time, Morgan has found that she's seeing the pattern within the melee before it happens, anticipating which one will come close first and what spin, duck, or twist she'll need to execute to eliminate them as efficiently as possible. It's like a movie where everything moves more slowly for her than for the bad guys. After wiping out scores of zombies easily, she's begun to slow down and study what injuries work best in the event she's ever at a huge disadvantage and needs to be even more surgical. While mortal wounds are only catastrophic injuries to the head or heart area—say a shotgun blast scarcely within arms' reach … messy, that one—a zombie can be debilitated like a human by breaking bones in the legs, such as shattering the knees or ankles, though the persistent bastards will then continue to crawl with grasping hands when they've been damaged far beyond what a normal person can bear.

Then come the days where she "forgets" a certain weapon at home, though, of course, it's an intentional oversight, like forgetting to reply to an overdue email or neglecting to take the trash cans out when you really do remember that it needs to be done but try to trick yourself into thinking you've forgotten. Forgetting on purpose. Nothing really significant, just a trick people have done to themselves for ages. *Whoops, forgot the shotgun today*, she thinks. *I should go back to the house and grab it … nah, I'm almost there, so I'll just make do*. She's fortunate that she's so physically gifted— as she has been her entire life … lucky *and* gifted. By late summer, she's taken trips where only one weapon has made it into the Jeep, but she's managed to survive the handful of skirmishes she initiated in this or that suburb of the city.

This is how Morgan spends the next few months of warm weather and through late fall—wake up, eat something for breakfast, drive to somewhere she hasn't been before, kill as many of them as she can find, stop for lunch, wipe more out in the afternoon, and then go home to a hot shower and romance novel. The count of double-dead corpses begins to rival those of the one time fallen as she scours the countryside and leaves wide swaths of permanent death in her wake by the many, *many* hundreds as the months accumulate.

Ah yes, her other guilty pleasure, aside from horror movies: romance novels. She doesn't remember the name

of the one that got her hooked since even she'll admit they
tend to blur together, but the recurring theme of them just
grabbed her. As marginally written as many of the bustier-
bursting books are, she devours them mainly because of her
longing for an equal. She wants to desire someone as much
as the men who have pursued her over the years desired her.
The women in the books seem to find that so easily and
fall into wonderful, sweaty, passionate stories she just can't
put down. Back when everyone else was alive, she checked
several romance books out at a time at the library, but then
she'd hide them in her vehicle so no one knew she was
reading them. She would also never let anyone accompany
her to the library. Her pattern had been to toss a few books
into her pack whenever she went on a hike, stop at the peak
of a hill in a bright, sunny spot, and read for hours until
it was time to return home. Now, she takes them out with
abandon—since all the librarians are dead too—and leaves
them scattered throughout the house once finished. She has
always desperately wanted to find a man who is her physical
peer as a mate, fascinates her psychologically, and meets her
never-ending drive to be moving, doing, and dominating
everything. Someone like her brother, but obviously not him.

Her brother!

The thought strikes her like a physical blow to her chest.

She's been so self-absorbed (not unusual) and wrapped
up in hunting and killing—new but getting a bit tedious if
she has to admit it—that it hasn't crossed her mind that he
may still be alive. After all, he's nearly as physically capable
as she is and, of course, is bigger and, therefore, more

powerful. He's also bright and resourceful. Could he have survived too? Charlotte is a huge city like Denver, so the odds aren't great since the hordes of zombies in big cities must be overwhelming, but he *is* out in the suburbs in that golf community. If he's alive, though, there's only one place he'll be: the lake. It's remote, quiet, and cold, which makes it an advantage in the winter. It's also utterly familiar ground to him since they've explored every inch of the area over the years. He will surely be drawn there by the fond childhood memories she knows he's kept in his greedy clutches as a salve for the difficult times of adulthood.

What should she do? She's bored with what she's doing every day—the challenge is frankly limited at this point, and she has nothing else to keep her here other than a super, self-sustaining house. What harm would there be in going cross-country to the lake to see if he's there? It will take a few days at most, and she can always come back if she wants, though the lake holds a few fond memories of her childhood as well—it was there that she had been free to race around the calm surface of the cool water with her brother, outdoors and away from the disapproving adults. She decides on the spot, as her eyes heavily fall toward sleep, to prepare over the next day or two and then head east. A different car will be nice too—the Jeep would be fine but not necessarily fun on the highways.

***

While Morgan sleeps, however, Mother Nature pushes into the area with the spectacular storm that drops more than two feet of snow overnight before moving east and visiting Pennsylvania and New York to surprise her brother and his companions. Armchair climatologists would have had a field day with the post-people weather as the cooling of the cities and all things man-made leads to a much colder winter than all the years before, lending weight to the global warming concerns that are now not such a concern. She isn't going anywhere, and she'll find that out in a few hours.

In the meantime, we'll leave Morgan behind to her quiet winter largely spent indoors exercising with weights and on the treadmill in the basement gym, training for survival. East is indeed our destination, where we need to catch up with a friend.

Part II: Eve

CHAPTER 4

Fall 2013

E ve stands in the warm sunlight and watches the truck loaded full of her companions and their supplies recede into the distance. She's torn between dashing madly down the street, waving her arms for them to come back and begging them to take her with them, and staying until her father dies. The knowledge that this is what they all have to do leaves a bitter feeling in her stomach.

The rumble of the exhaust begins to fade just as she hears the zombies' call carry across the water of the lake behind her, like the echo of a faraway thunderstorm. A frisson of fear dances a delicate pirouette down her spine as the realization that she's truly alone and unprotected for the first time in months sinks in, and she ducks quickly back into the house, locking the heavy front door behind her.

Alone, save for the dying man and the ever-present threat of zombies.

Alone and frightened.

She walks back through the foul-smelling house—not really *home*, not any longer—wrinkling her nose at the glowering odor of her father's sickness, wanting nothing more than to open all the windows and allow some fresh air to sweep the pollution of what she pictures as microscopic black particles of illness floating among the dust motes out into the beyond. Eve has always been a duty-bound person, always doing the right or expected thing, making the safe choices, and rarely taking risks throughout her more than thirty years of life. The new reality is a shocking change for her, and she is amazed she has survived out of luck's random choice.

Not to mention being delivered to someone who's been so capable of watching over you and the rest of the group, her own inner voice reminds her.

The traditional route of college, then work, then marriage to a nice, safe, ordinary man, basically just having a "normal life," has been her path, aside from a short and confusing dalliance with a professor during her later college years. She's had the same impulses as anyone else to make poor decisions, but she's also chosen the obvious path almost every time. The decision to stay behind while the other three continue on their journey seemed a straightforward one—it's her father, and he brought her into the world and raised her to be a good person; it's her responsibility to be there to shepherd him in some measure of comfort during his finishing journey. Now, however, the reality of being by herself with him and the fact that he's going to die soon and leave her truly alone in the middle of basically nowhere starts to sink in heavily and she wonders—not for the last time—if she has made the right decision for herself. She knows she can follow her friends as soon as he dies, though she recoils a bit at the idea of driving to a strange place on her own.

Taking a few moments to meander through the house, she checks all the windows and doors to ensure they're fastened, though she resolves to open some of the higher windows for a short time since the smell threatens to overwhelm her.

Passing her childhood room and a sequence of fading family photos aligned in a descending row on the lightly oiled wood paneling of the hallway, she arrives at the threshold of her father's room. She stops quietly, watching and listening, but he's resting peacefully, his breathing even and painless. A minute passes as she absently watches him sleep, and then she turns and makes her way back down the hall to do ... something. Not quite sure what, but something to fill the time, as she fears her father will hold on for a long time. She then immediately feels guilty for the thought.

She has never been a homebody, preferring to be physically active at something other than chores, but she needs something to occupy her time. She sets about cleaning the house. Dust cloaks every surface in a dull, sticky shroud; she tackles that task first, stirring the motes, which flicker into life in the rays of sunlight making their way in through the cloudy windows. Finishing that, she finds a container of glass cleaner underneath the kitchen sink and scrubs the panes until they shine clear. The old battery-powered clock over the refrigerator tracks her progress with endless soft ticks, and while she feels as though she's been busy for many hours, she realizes only a couple have passed when she looks up from the final window. Eve is grateful for the mindless tasks since they take her mind off her predicament.

Why stay? Duty? Love? Both?

Yes.

Growing up, she was close with her family, like any ordinary kid, and as an only child, she benefited from undivided attention from her parents. They had attended every function, even golf, as her abilities had grown to the point of receiving an All State award in high school. They'd dutifully trudged along for eighteen holes, her father making minor gestures to hint at what had gone wrong when she'd made a mistake and flashing a cheerful thumbs-up when she'd made a good shot. Yes, love binds her to the house, though, in this new reality, she knows it's a foolish choice since her father's death sentence is evident in his drawn visage. Who knows how long he'll live or how she'll react when the end comes. She just knows that whenever it does, she'll follow the rest of the group to the lake cabins in New York. That's their destination, and she fervently hopes they are there already, safe and sound.

Vacuuming is needed as well, though without electricity, that isn't an option. So after she cleans the very few dishes and glasses in the sink with some of the bottled water her companions left behind along with food and weapons, she finds herself without something to do next. Even after going several months without power, she still has trouble making the adjustment, catches herself flipping light switches as she enters a darker room out of habit. Glancing out the window, she looks at the fading sun reflecting off the lake and sees that her mother's carefully crafted and meticulously maintained gardens have run to riot with weeds and overgrowth. So she puts it on her mental list to clean them up, though she realizes being exposed outdoors and engrossed in a task doesn't seem particularly wise.

After looking in on her father (still sleeping, good), she drifts into her childhood bedroom and falls gently into the memories trapped therein. Her myriad golf awards dot the walls and bookshelves, a glistening army of golden statues frozen midswing that memorialize her young career in the most complicated sport ever invented. There are old photos from her high school or earlier years, faded from time, recalling best friends and boyfriends, smiling children with no inkling that life will end horribly for most of them just over a decade later. Her gaze lingers on a picture of Bobby Stone, her most serious high school boyfriend ... well, as serious as one can be during that time. He smiles back at her from their junior year prom photo, he in a now ridiculous white tuxedo with tails and pink cummerbund, she in a pink dress bound with a white belt of ribbon at her midsection. He was a sweet boy—they really were all just boys then, not men, despite the posturing and attempted toughness that comes with adolescence—member of the boys' golf team, with his lanky limbs, pimples, and an anxious fascination with anything to do with sex. Fumbling encounters in the back of his father's Mustang convertible slip into her mind, and she grins softly at the recollection of those sweaty, nervous, and of course, fun memories.

As her eyes flit across the miniature frozen view of her history, there in the background of another photo from a Friday night football game, eye black smeared across his shining, sweaty cheeks, is Alex Jameson, her high school crush. Unlike Bobby, who was a straight-A student, polite, and cautious, Alex was the typical high school bad boy. A star linebacker for the football team with a wicked grin, an edgy sense of humor, and a wild streak, he was the one all the girls mooned over and he knew it. Eve had admired him for years, watching the way his muscles rippled under the ratty T-shirt he always wore for practices as he ran with the grace and speed of a gazelle across the sprawling football field. He'd been aware of her lingering gazes, and one evening, following a huge upset win against a longtime rival, he found her beneath the bleachers, took her hand, steered her deeper into the shadows away from the postgame throng, and kissed her hotly among the discarded popcorn containers, scraps of candy wrappers, and empty water bottles. She remembers thinking, *Why me out of all the girls in the school who have the hots for him?*

What Eve hadn't known about herself then, and has not learned since, is that despite her nice but average looks, her sensuality surrounds her in a halo of subtle decadence. Many men have arduously pursued her over the years—ones she's always thought were out of her league—because she smolders with a sensuality in every gesture that inexorably beckons. She's completely unaware that she has this effect, and while men take a moment or two to initially notice her, once they do, she draws their returning gaze with unfaltering magnetism, hence the problem with Jack and the college professor, the burning kiss with Alex, and numerous others over the years. Something in the way she looks directly at people and the combination of her reserved nature, petite figure, strong will, and porcelain skin makes men desire her, and most of them struggle with defining why she's so achingly attractive.

Even now, she could still feel the smooth skin of Alex's young face as though it were pressing urgently against hers, the twist of his tongue in her mouth. She had broken the embrace off when his hand had begun to slide up her sweater, knowing Bobby would be heartbroken if he ever found out, and there was no future with Alex. As was his nature, he'd move on to the next girl without batting an eye once he'd gotten what he clearly wanted from Eve, and she'd be left with nothing. He got angry when she broke the kiss and tried kissing her again, more roughly than before, and she pushed him sharply away from her and ran off to rejoin the crowd filtering back to their cars.

Stunned to find herself blushing hard at the recollection of the first and only kiss with Alex, Eve pulls her eyes away from the photo. He never paid her another speck of attention after that incident and spent the rest of their high school years chasing cheerleaders and being the life of parties held at the remote edges of the lake. The unspoken rejection stung her delicate teenage emotions for many months thereafter, and she often found herself shamefully thinking of him when she was with Bobby, wondering, *What if I hadn't stopped him?*

At the close of high school, as is typical, everyone went their separate ways to scattered colleges and universities, and they all lost track of one another. Bobby had received a partial golf scholarship to a school in the South—she can't recall which one—and never returned to Lake Ariel. They'd parted amicably enough, saying all the things high school sweethearts say when separating for college, and diligently wrote nightly emails for a few months before trailing off and stopping before the winter break. Alex had gone to Florida State—how she remembers his college over Bobby's, she doesn't know—to play football, and the town threw a late-summer brouhaha to send him off since he was going to put Lake Ariel on the map once he realized his athletic dreams. The hero worship didn't last long, nor did Lake Ariel land on the public consciousness.

Eve's mother had been a constant source of information and was somehow more up to date than Facebook, and some years ago, she told Eve that Alex had blown a knee out in his sophomore season, robbing him of his speed and explosiveness and thereby ending any NFL dreams. She also told Eve, not without some of the glee that comes with all gossip about the misfortunes of others, that he'd returned to town, begun working at his father's car dealership, and "married that June Everham girl and gotten himself fat."

Eve drags herself out of her memories, leaves them behind, and falls into one of the armchairs in the family room. She feels trapped in the house, the walls closing in on her, and it has only been a single day. Tears leaking from her eyes, she whispers a prayer that her father will die soon and cries heavily for some time for a lot of reasons. She can't remember ever being so miserable in her life.

***

Her father doesn't die quickly, however. As the weather continues to cool and bring the clarity of fall, both in the air and in the sky as the leaves abandon their posts and broaden the view across the lake, he clings to life with the tenacity of a wino fiercely gripping his last bottle, clutching it stubbornly to his chest. His condition doesn't vary much; he sleeps most of each day, waking only for spotty periods of lucidity, during which they talk about the far past of his or her youth or the more recent ferocious events where everyone's world has been wiped away without time for a deep breath.

He fills her in on what happened in the town when the wave of zombies had come through. He'd had the benefit of a good pension from a job on a railroad and only recently retired to enjoy time at home with his wife after nearly four decades of work. Like throughout the rest of the world, there was almost no warning before the onslaught of bloody terror crashed into the quiet town and most of the population was dead—or a new member of Team Zombie—within twenty-four hours. A number of the few initial survivors rapidly gathered weapons, food, and water and barricaded themselves in one of the local churches that sat just off the town square. With high windows well above ground level, heavy oak double doors, and the single steel emergency exit door in the back of the building, it was easily secured ... or so they thought. A balcony just four rows deep for seating ran in a squared U around the perimeter of the second floor, with large windows that afforded both a clear line of sight and an excellent shooting position. The thirty or so of them were forced to witness the town succumb to the horror of people running, fighting, and dying right in front of their eyes. Swarms of zombies came through, systematically searched all the buildings to flush out any of the remaining residents, and then fell on them in a terrible melee of biting, tearing, screaming, and suffering.

Just like in North Carolina with the queen as their leader and on the drive here with the alpha in the mountain pass, Eve thinks. She asks her father more about that, whether there had been a leading zombie.

"Yes," he replies. A "man" had been in the center of all the monsters, directing them here and there with gestures, clearly in command of the rest of the shambling, single-minded morass. Her father's group tried to pick off the zombie leader from one of the windows, which was a fatal mistake. Until then, the churchgoers had gone unnoticed from the outside—they'd taken care to avoid standing in the windows during the day and hadn't risked light in the dark hours, just observed from the corners of windows. One of the neighbors from their street, Mr. Thompson, a professor at a nearby college and resident know-it-all, had gathered the people together once they'd realized there was a leader who was coordinating a step-by-step assassination of all remaining humans. He explained that if they killed the zombie leader, maybe the rest of them would move along. It wouldn't solve the obvious problem of the entire world being overrun by the abominations of nature—or was this man's fault? A virus? Genetic experimentation gone insanely wrong?—but it would maybe buy them some space and time in their little corner of it. After all, when the world is coming to an end, any extra time to do anything is good time to have.

It was early evening when they tried. The zombies gathered in a loose audience in the center of the town each day to be dispatched hither and yon by their ringleader. As the group watched most of the zombies scatter throughout the streets and farther into the outskirts, they slid a balcony window open, and one of the town's hunters eased himself into a decent shooting position. It was maybe one hundred yards; no reason for a good shooter to miss at that kind of range, but he did, and the shot splattered the head of the next zombie over.

Ten heads covered in oily hair, gore, dirt, and whatever else they'd picked up swiveled in unison and fixed their eyes on the church. The leader immediately pulled several of the other zombies in front of him, completely shielding himself from a second attempt. Their hunter was frozen for a costly moment in shock after realizing he'd missed and lost his opportunity. No sound from the group, but they dispersed quickly to get under cover and surrounded the church in a hungry cordon, with others from the scouting teams pouring in from between buildings to thicken the barrier.

There was nowhere to go; the people indoors could see they were completely encircled, and a quick peek out the back door confirmed no exit possible there. It was time to fight and probably die, but like Americans of legend, most of the group gathered themselves for an act of stubborn bravery and checked weapons, shook hands with one another, hugged and kissed their spouses if present, and picked a window. A few, including the professor, drifted off deeper into the shadows within the building to vanish cowardly in the hopeful darkness. Eve's father and mother stationed themselves at adjacent windows and quietly promised each other they wouldn't allow their deaths to be by zombie.

Then there was a howling call that sent bullets of fear into humans the world over.

Muuuuuuuhhhhh!

They came at the building in a rush, before the defenders could squeeze many shots off, and without much ado or fancy strategy, simply using the weight of their collective bodies to push through the front doors. The doors opened out, as do those of most public buildings. They had been fashioned out of thick oak, darkened by generations of staining by both the care of human hands and Mother Nature, and were completely sturdy, capable of stopping a bullet. Their frame, however, was weakened by some termite infestation decades ago. The termites had been eliminated, but the tunnels scoured into the wood by the insects combined with the ensuing years of weather betrayed the people inside. Hinges of the now pulpy frame tore loose, and the doors fell inward with a crash onto the stacked rear pews, like a giant-sized bowling ball clearing the pins. There was a pause from both groups as they all stood there and sized one another up, and more than one human felt their bowels weaken or heart quiver. The zombies around the back of the building poured around the sides and created a queue at the fallen doors not unlike those on a typical—though far less messy—Sunday morning.

With a surge, the zombies exploded into the ground floor, clambering over the debris of the doors, staggering over the benches, and clearing a path for those behind. There were well over fifty of them now, and the weak souls who had sought refuge on the ground floor in the shadows died horribly, screaming in pain as they were devoured alive, pleading with their fellow residents and for the God who had abandoned them to come help them. Those in the balcony fired their guns into the seething mass below them at will, muzzle flashes lighting the building from every direction. An onlooker from outside would have thought there was a party indoors save for the howls of dying humans and sickening grunts of those eating them.

It didn't take long for the horde to find the stairs on either side of the front doors that led to the balcony. The remaining people had a brief, perfect bottleneck to shoot at as the horde came one at a time through the upper doorway, but they were quickly overwhelmed by the volume. Despite their bravery, those poor people had never had to fight for their lives, nor were most of them accurate enough for the requisite head shots. The tide turned within a minute or two as the zombies erupted into the space and began taking their toll in sheets of blood.

Her father stops at this point in the tale, just drifting into silence as he recalls that night of death and loss. Eve waits as his eyes leave the room and look again into the not-too-distant past.

After a few moments, he draws in a shuddering breath and finishes the tale.

There was no escape by going over the balcony rail and into the roiling scene on the ground floor. Shattered pews and bodies lay askew and prevented any chance of a safe landing, let alone a passage to the outdoors. Their only chance was jumping out one of the windows, which was over fifteen feet above the ground. Her parents were both in their midsixties, and while they'd stayed active over the years, age carried its own risk. He told Eve it was her mother who said they had to jump—anything was better than the certain death creeping down the aisles of God with yawning mouths of gore. He continued to fire his shotgun into the mass of bodies looming toward them as she opened the window and eased onto the ledge to try and reduce the height of the fall. Once she dropped, he followed with two more blasts and then jumped into the darkness, lit only occasionally now by the strobes of the weakening gunfire within the church.

His wife's groan of pain helped him find her crawling off to the left, and he hurried to her side while scanning their perimeter for danger. A broken left ankle twisted her foot at an unnatural angle, and she was in misery. Amid her tears of fear and pain, he hoisted her into a standing position with an arm over his shoulder and began to hobble off into the depths of the shadows and safety. They could find another place to hide, somewhere to hole up and wrap the injury, and then maybe escape what was left of the town. All they needed was a minute of going unnoticed.

They didn't get it.

Muuuuuuuhhhhh!

A half dozen of the zombies, led by the one they'd seen giving directions, came around the corner of the building, lurching along in their inexorable gait that wasn't fast but seemed to cover ground more efficiently than it looked. The couple hopped along for a few dozen desperate yards when she stopped him, telling him to just go, run, get away, leave her.

"No," he'd said to his partner of thirty-five years, "there is no way I'm leaving you behind!"

"You have to! If we stay together, we both die. If you leave me, you have a chance to live. Find Eve and get away! We don't have time to fight about this!"

She firmly pushed him away from her and raised her pistol to fire into the closing line of zombies, trying to shoot the leader and buy them some space. She was a strong-willed, independent, and practical woman who was not one to linger over decisions when they had to be made.

"I can't leave you! Come with me. We can make it," he'd pleaded with her.

"You're right—you can't leave me to die at their hands. You made a promise in the house of God. Keep it!"

He stops the tale again, tears pouring freely out of his eyes.

"Daddy," she says, reverting to the inner child who never goes completely away and wants comfort and solace from their parent, her own stinging tears racing down her face; she's afraid to ask the next question but knows there's no way not to. "What happened?"

He doesn't respond right away, just holds her gaze for several quiet moments before replying. "Does it matter? Either way, she's gone, and I have to carry the guilt with me for the rest of my life. I'm glad that won't be for much longer." With that, he closes his tearful eyes and turns away from her, vaguely waving a hand to dismiss her from the room and give him the privacy he needs to relive the last moments of his wife's life … however it had ended, since only he knows.

Eve was wrong about her level of misery earlier. As she leaves the room, she can't tear her mind off the picture now painted with shocking clarity in her mind of what that night had been like for her parents and what it might have been like to have to make that decision. She pauses in the hallway and looks back at his room, wondering if her father is dying of an actual sickness or something else. Guilt?

Praying to her own rather intangible version of a higher being, she asks to never be faced with such a decision and aftermath. She dodges the thought creeping into her mind about what she would have done if it had been her husband in that situation, as their short-lived marriage had forged nothing like the bond her parents had. She pushes the thought away as firmly as her father expelled her from the room—some things are better just not considered.

***

The problem, though, with thoughts like that is they linger in the corners of the mind, in the deep closets where they've been tucked away, and then jump out just for fun.

Surprise! Here I am, some shit you really don't want to ponder. No, no, you're not dodging me, no. I'm going to sit here in the fringes of what you really want to think about and poke at you. I'll be here, right where you don't want me. All week folks, all week.

Eve hasn't been aware of how much the clutter of the world's noise and nonsense has gotten in the way of actual thinking. The distraction of the most current onslaught of "incredible, amazing, super, cannot-be-missed thingy" and "pictures of cute animals or fucked-up celebrities or world's most amazing, not-to-be-missed whatever" shortened everyone's attention span and attention to details. Like connections with humans details. It had been pretty quiet in North Carolina after everything since there had only been the four of them, or five for a blessedly short period of time—another thought that won't disappear: What *really* happened to Jack, and did she care? But now the depths of silence are stunningly dark, like being inside a cave and having your flashlight batteries suddenly die. No matter how much you shake it, dead batteries are dead batteries, billions of dead people are dead people, and any sound she makes does little to the deafeningly mute voice of the world.

All quiet on every front.

Eve remembers talking about this very thing with *him* when it was just the two of them at first. They were reading on the porch in the sun and talking about how both of them are comfortable with quiet, how that particular change isn't horrible, and how they're both watchers and listeners, absorbing far more than those around them realize. She misses him already, along with Amelie and DeeDee. But there's all the time in the world to wander down that path too.

Eve spends the next few weeks alternating between spending her time taking an inglorious romp down memory lane, both the childhood and more recent one, caring for her father, and wondering what has happened to her companions. The weather has burrowed itself firmly in very late fall, and the air has begun to smell like threatening snow at times. As she spends more time in her head than is recommended, she comes to a lukewarm realization that her life has been fine. Just fine … that's it. Her marriage had been nice enough but bland. It was okay when he was there; it was okay when he was not. Their love life had been fine whether it was on or off, and her days had been acceptable whether they were spent on the golf course or writing or exercising or hanging around with her friends, but they had all been like Groundhog Day—they were pretty much all the same, no spikes, no valleys. That realization is paired with another one that she has known it all along, which then leads to the trifecta that she has been a passive person for far too long and should have done something about it. While those waters of the past are already well under the bridge and can't be changed, she resolves that, going forward, she'll do what she wants to do, not what everyone else thinks is the "right thing" to do—not that there are a lot of everyones left. There's no way of knowing how much is left in the story of her life, but she's going to live the next chapter on her own terms. The thought gives her some strength, and she pulls her shoulders back and lifts her head a little higher.

***

That chapter starts soon thereafter. Most mornings, Eve awakens with the dawn, shrugs on some clothes—some of which, she's noted with a small measure of pride, are from her teenage years and still fit … mostly—checks the house, scans the area through the windows to ensure she has no visitors, and then turns on the side burner of the grill on the back porch to make instant coffee as she overlooks the calming waters of the still lake.

Once the coffee is ready, she leans against the doorjamb and peeks in on her father, watching him through the rising steam from the mug, trying to measure the difference from the day before, if there is any.

This morning begins like any other, same routine. Her father is peaceful and still, and it takes her a few minutes to realize with a small start that he isn't moving. No rise and fall of his chest, no small movements of his hands or head.

Gone.

Just like that.

She doesn't need to walk over and check his pulse or anything. Now that she's more aware, she can see the faded pallor of his skin, the shrunken features of his face as they must've sagged in after he drew his final breath. Eve simply accepts it. No tears, no raging at the unfairness of life. This version of the world is just as fair as the one that had come before it.

It isn't.

She knew this was coming from the moment she first walked into his room and saw his condition. It was just a matter of when and how, and she's thankful that it appears to have been peaceful. No grimace on his face … just gone. There's no expression on her own face as she stands there sipping the rest of her coffee, looking at him without a single thought in her mind. There's time for other things later.

She just takes a moment.

CHAPTER 5

Eve spends the rest of the day moving aimlessly around the house, trying to figure out what to do next. Just leave? Head for the lake where her friends are? Stay, bury her father, and decide what to do later? Sit on the fence and do nothing? Get ragingly drunk? All of the above?

Get drunk, bury her father, head for the other lake.

That's it.

***

That isn't it.

The same early and mammoth storm that howls across the lake in New York hits Lake Ariel first, so as she sits in the shadows of the kitchen with a heavy crystal tumbler of whiskey, sipping steadily away at her grief—which is less than she expected; she already largely mourned her parents before coming here—and feeling the vague blur grow into a rather pleasant and dense fog, the snow quietly arrives. A few more fingers of whiskey and a couple of hours of the white stuff later, Eve is sprawled askew on the table, head down on her left arm, with an unladylike drip of saliva drifting from her mouth. She isn't going anywhere anytime soon, but she doesn't know that. She just sleeps, rests, and closes the chapter of the last remnant of her life before.

***

She awakes to a headache crafted of grinding shards of glass mixed with nails being shaken inside the aluminum can of her head. After a few painful attempts, she finally manages to open her eyes cautiously and sees the massive accumulation of snow (that's still rising) on the back deck of the house. None of the survivors could know this since all the weathermen are, ahem, "under the weather," but the winter is to be one of the coldest on record—though no one is keeping track of records—over the last century, dropping more snow more often than even any remaining old-timers, shivering in their own hideouts, can recall. Earth is cooler now that the countless millions of heat-producing engines and, of course, most of man- and womankind have come to a stop. No one will ever find out if global warming is real, but global everybody-just-died-and-turned-off-several-billion-small-heat-generators-and-all-their-gadgets makes an almost instantaneous difference on the climate. Unfortunately for those in the already colder parts of the world, which are a bit more zombie-proof than the temperate climes—Florida, for example, quickly becomes a mob of zombie families wandering around the theme parks looking for food inside that mouse or duck costume, and skinny, augmented, bikini-clad zombies patrolling South Beach—the cold makes for a really shitty, long winter.

Eve is not nearly as prepared as those in New York, though there's a woodburning fireplace in the house and hopefully enough wood to make things at least bearable through the cold weather. She thinks she'll have to gather more of it from throughout the neighboring areas. And she has the little problem of the corpse in the back bedroom that needs to be taken care of. All of this is overwhelming and unsettling her, and all she really wants to do is go back to sleep and pretend none of this happened, which would be nice except for those drinks of whiskey ….

And now, ladies and gentlemen, if I can direct your attention to the young woman regurgitating what little is in her stomach over yonder porch railing ….

***

A good while later, Eve is settled enough emotionally and physically to consider the problem of her father. She makes a small fire in the fireplace, not thinking about the smoke from the chimney. The flames comfort her more due to the memories of sitting here in this spot as a child with her parents rather than the meager warmth they initially provide. Proper burial is out of the question due to the snow and the fact that there isn't any way she can dig a real hole on her own, and she doesn't want to leave his body exposed for animals to get into.

After some consideration, she decides that the best thing to do is move him to one of the neighboring houses. So she begins the process of getting him out of the stinking bed and bedroom by untucking the fitted sheet from the corners and dragging him to the edge of the bed. Not being strong enough to lift the body properly—nor really inclined to touch him more than absolutely necessary—she lowers him onto another comforter on the floor and then wraps it all around him before sliding him along the dark hallway toward the front door. One of his hands slumps out of the ad hoc sleeping bag to trail along the hardwood, so she stops and hesitantly tucks it back in before continuing. Part of her mind keeps dancing to the idea that he's going to suddenly sit up with the blanket still covering his face and ask her what on earth she's doing or, even worse, howl that miserable noise the zombies make and begin to chase her around the house. Eve pushes that thought away as much as she can. Not that her father would have been able to help her had something happened, but his presence has at least been comforting for the notion of not being alone. She's now very cognizant of being alone in the middle of fucking nowhere. Little spiders of panic are walking delicately on the fringes of the web of her consciousness, and she finds she suddenly can't settle her heart rate.

Great. I'm going to have a heart attack while I'm dragging my dead father out into two feet of snow by myself to stash him in a hopefully empty house like a side of beef. You can't make this stuff up.

She sits down hard in the hallway, sobbing and shaking, frightened.

She takes another moment.

***

More hours sneak by while she sleeps, resting against the wall under a twenty-year-old photo of her parents in tennis attire—sweatbands, headbands, alarmingly shiny short shorts, and broad, young, alive smiles. It's almost completely dark outside (and inside) now, with the fire having burned down to a barely glowing bed of scowling embers and the heavy cloud cover obscuring the scant illumination of the moon.

It's deep twilight when she wakes up and recalls where she is and what she's been doing. The sleep has calmed her down, so she stands up shakily at first and stoops back to the task so she can get it over with. She drags her father the rest of the way to the front stairs, whispers a soft, "Sorry, Daddy," and pulls him as gently as she can down the three steps to the front door, doing absolutely everything she can to ignore the dull thump of his skull knocking against the steps. Opening the door and allowing a shocking gust of cold air into the house, Eve steps back onto the front stoop and pulls hard against the blanket to cross the threshold and into the resistance of the deep snow.

"Need a hand with that?"

CHAPTER 6

Eve promptly loses her grip on the blanket, and almost all that's left of her tentative grip on her sanity in that moment, and falls backward into the heavy snow to land painfully on her backside. Now more frightened than she has been since her friends left, she looks up and around her in the darkening air for the source of the voice, which had been deep and male. A flashlight flares to life, showing a pair of dark brown boots below blue jeans, and then a pale hand emerges from the darkness to reach for her.

"Here, let me help you up. I'm sorry I startled you," the voice continues. It sounds nice enough. In a way, it sounds like the voice of a smaller man, which makes her feel less threatened, but she still hesitates, feeling the cold snow beneath her hands begin to melt and her fingers start to become numb.

"Lady, are you going to just sit there in the snow getting wet and cold? My mom said that was the best way to catch a cold, you know." A child's voice. Female. Not a really young one, but maybe in her early teens?

"It's okay," comes the man's voice again. "We're not going to hurt you. We smelled the smoke from your chimney across town and came to find out who else had survived."

Eve pauses for one more moment and then reaches up to the still-outreached hand and stands as he tugs her back to an upright position. She's suddenly aware that she's very cold and hasn't really thought out her wardrobe for being outside, though she also hasn't been planning on having company or being outdoors for very long. Crossing her cold arms over the thin T-shirt that's covering her chest, she looks at her visitors without speaking. The fading sunset and flashlight's glow holds just enough light for her to get a good look as her eyes adjust to the gloom.

The man is tallish, lean, and in his middle forties, perhaps, with a blue knit cap covering what looks like a thinning head of hair. A sharp Roman nose protrudes from a face covered in several weeks' worth of beard and topped by a pair of dark eyes that are studying her as well. He's wearing a bulky wool hunting jacket of black and red squares and the jeans and boots she's already seen from below. No threat appears to lurk within his eyes, just a fairly ordinary-looking man.

Just behind him stands the girl who'd spoken. She's a thin little thing who looks no more than twelve or thirteen, cloaked in a long overcoat wrapped tightly around her and draped down to the tops of dingy, white sneakers that must provide no warmth. No hat; a wild nest of blonde hair pokes out in all directions, like something a child would do when trying to draw hair on a person for the first time. She's wearing green, fingerless gloves and clutches the coat tightly around her.

"I'm Ned. This," the man says, with a part turn to the girl, "is Amy."

Amy … Amelie.

It hits her instantly. Similar ages, both survivors. Her mind flips to her companions, and she suddenly and desperately wishes they were here, both for company and for the protection they provided.

Eve has a decision to make: turn these strangers away or welcome them in.

The child decides that coin toss. "Lady, can you talk? I'm cold, Ned. I want to go inside, somewhere. What's inside that blanket anyway?"

Eve can practically hear the poor girl's teeth chattering as she speaks, and so she finally finds her own voice. "Eve. My name is Eve. This is, *was* my father. I need to … bury him."

"Well, Eve, it's nice to meet you. That's a pretty name, by the way. How about Amy goes inside to warm up, and you and I take care of your father? Would that be okay?"

Eve nods and gestures to the partly open front door, and Amy quickly bustles past her, shedding her shoes as she steps through the threshold of the house, and quickly vanishes around the edge of the door. Ned looks at her for a moment and then bends down to collect one end of the blanket. Eve does the same at the other end, and they hoist her father, walk awkwardly through the depths of the snow to the house next door, find the basement unlocked (and unoccupied), and lay her father to rest in a summery lounge chair. After Ned stands back respectfully, Eve makes sure her father is completely covered and then closes her eyes, lowers her head, and whispers a quiet prayer that he will be joining her mother wherever it is souls go, if anywhere. When she opens her eyes, she finds Ned staring at her more directly than she likes in the glow of the flashlight, and she's again conscious of the cold, her light clothing, and her solitude. Suddenly, he smiles brightly at her and says they should get indoors where it's warm and safe.

They spend the next few hours getting warm food into the three of them, chatting lightly, and figuring out sleeping arrangements. No one is going to sleep in her father's ruined bed, so Eve's in her own room, Amy's on a day bed in the third bedroom, and Ned's on the couch near the fireplace. He brought the fire back to a comforting roar after they'd come indoors, so he seems to be very capable. Eve had quickly found a light sweater and shrugged it on over her thin shirt, but nothing else that evening throws her radar up. Still, with thoughts of Jack not long in the past, she pauses when she closes her door for bedtime and then quietly turns the lock.

The rules are different now, after all.

There are none.

***

Eve awakens with a start the next morning from the fog of a deep sleep after hearing noises in the house. She is suddenly terrified she had forgotten to lock the door and a zombie or two have gotten in and she's moments away from a messy death. Just as her panicked mind starts to urge her to move a dresser in front of the door and then climb out the window and make a run for it in her pajamas, she hears the murmur of conversation from the kitchen, and it all snaps into place. The clink of silverware against a mug, the bubbling of unintelligible words alternating between male and female voices.

She has company.

She slips out from under the heavy blankets, shrugs some clothes on—including an extra layer; the house is cold and … well, you know—and makes her way out to join them. Ned greets her with a grin and hands her a steaming cup of fresh coffee. Amy looks up from a photo album and mumbles something like "good morning," sounding like someone who has been awakened earlier than she prefers. She's holding on to a mug of what must have been hot chocolate.

Once they've had a scant breakfast of dry and mostly stale cereal, Ned and Eve settle at the kitchen table for some more detailed introductions. As they do so, she realizes the provisions she has in the house won't be nearly enough to sustain the three of them, but she pushes the thought to the side for the moment since it means action, which can wait—plus, there's the crapload of snow everywhere too. Eve gives Ned her backstory, starting from when the zombies came, though excludes the uglier details of Jack. Besides, while she suspects Jack's demise was truly at the hands (or mouths) of zombies, she also suspects that it wasn't quite that simple.

Ned quickly runs through his own history. He was an independent accountant for many of the small businesses in the area as well as a shade tree mechanic specializing in vintage BMWs and had grown up and lived just a few towns over. Unmarried, no other attachments or relatives, just a simple life. He had been visiting a client for their annual audit when the initial wave of zombies poured over the gentle towns spotting the area, scouring the humans from the face of the Earth in vast swaths of agony and blood. He went into hiding immediately. Like most other survivors, once the furor of the first week or so ended and things quieted down, he went about securing a safe place to live, food and water supplies, and weapons and then cautiously searched for others while on the never-ending lookout for the horde. He discovered Amy shortly thereafter, hiding in the corner of the basement of an otherwise empty house he'd been scavenging from. She was buried under a blanket, starving, dehydrated, and scared out of her mind. She was a foster child who had been placed in a neighboring family's home just recently, but she escaped when that house had been invaded and wandered aimlessly through the unfamiliar town until finding refuge behind the furnace in a too-small-for-zombies space.

"That's right," the girl pipes up from underneath a heavy blanket. "Ned's saving me." She goes back to flipping through the visual history of Eve's family. "You used to have funny hair," she adds, clearly having come across photos from the 1980s.

Ned explains that he brought Amy back to his hideout near the church in the town center and got her some food, water, and rest. Eve's mind flickers back to her "delivery," which went almost the same way—water, food, whiskey, and sleep.

The two of them have been together since then, just trying to live and find others and staying off the zombies' radar since there are still some roving packs in the area like the one Eve heard when her friends departed. Ned and Amy gathered firewood throughout the fall, but once the snow started, they raced to accumulate more and move some inside as well so they would have a dry supply. It was around that time they picked up the scent of Eve's fire, so they decided to make their way across town to investigate.

They come to a pause in the conversation after covering their respective pasts, but Ned fills it almost immediately. "Your friends and that place you're telling me they went to— they sound really nice and safer than here. And another girl for Amy to have as a companion? That would be really great." There's a tone in his voice that can only be described as longing that Eve is pleased to hear. It sounds like kindness, which is reassuring. "Are you going to go there, now that your father is … well, gone?"

"That's what I was planning on doing after my dad passed, and then the snow blew in here," Eve replies. "I think we're going to be stuck for a while since I imagine there is even more snow at their higher elevation." She knows there's another decision to be made, but she also realizes it was already made when she allowed the two of them into her house. "Do you two want to stay here with me until the weather clears, and we can go up there together?"

"Eve, thank you. That's what I was hoping you'd ask. We'd love to stay here and get to know you better. I'm *so* happy we found you. Isn't that right, Amy?" Ned wears a broad smile, and Eve finds herself smiling along with him.

"Sure, yup," Amy says. "It would be even better if they had Wi-Fi up there, don't you think? I miss using my phone. None of my apps work right anymore since, you know."

Ned looks at her with a wry grin and raises an eyebrow. Eve smiles right back with a little bit of a "kids these days" expression on her own face and feels content. She has a new group. She won't be alone when she travels to New York, and she even has something of a plan. That's a good thing. She also relinquishes her initial misgivings about Ned, chalking them up to the general weirdness of this new reality and Jack-inspired paranoia about most men of late.

***

Having company is going to be a grand thing in the months to come; like for her former companions up in New York, the beginning of a miserable winter is here, and they'll be spending a lot of time indoors waiting out the temperament of Mother Nature. Doing so in solitude would be a certain recipe for madness. Doing so together will be okay because nothing ominous ever gets thrown into tales right about here.

***

However, their winter is quiet too. Take away power and all the newer distractions of the world, and there's not a damn lot to keep people occupied. Heat is a priority of course, so they make many trips to the houses nearby to gather as much split wood as possible in order to keep the fireplace going twenty-four hours a day and the cloying cold somewhat at bay. All three of them scour the house and nearby homes for books to read, decks of cards, board games to play—though, after a month or so, Amy begins to refer to them as "bored games"—and additional supplies. Many spirited games of Monopoly and other classics are played, though Ned proves to be more clever than Eve originally gave him credit for, with a calculating mind behind his mild outer appearance. Plainly put, he kicks their asses at Monopoly and anything else to do with strategy.

At times, Eve feels like he enjoys victory a little too much, noting a gleam in his eyes if he outwits or outmaneuvers the two females, but she chalks it up to someone who once used his brain for a living and, therefore, revels in its sharpness. Other than that, he's polite and considerate, and if his gaze lingers a bit too long on her at times, she understands that too. It's a lonely new world; his looks don't carry the hunger that all adult women recognize as potentially dangerous—or thrilling, for some—so she feels secure in their small sanctuary since the deep cold also keeps the zombies off the list of things to worry about.

There's just a single thing she catches after it happens often enough for her to see the pattern: he's not at all paternalistic with Amy, which makes some sense since he's not her father. But while he's polite and considerate to her most of the time, he also orders her around a lot in mostly subtle ways, and his face will darken briefly if she's slow to act. Eve doesn't have much personal experience with children herself and knows that the current crop—well, what's left of them—are a bit more willful and independent than their predecessors have been. So she assumes his reaction is just the frustration of a relationship that doesn't work the way he thinks it should.

For her part, Eve finds that she enjoys taking care of someone, even doing simple tasks like preparing meals or keeping Amy distracted and occupied with a game of cards or idle chatter when the youngster is clearly bored and catching cabin fever. There's something rewarding in the role of provider that she's never experienced before, and she finds that she looks forward to those times and appreciates that they also keep her busy.

Always armed, the three of them take some early winter walks through the remnants of the modest downtown area. They rapidly quit those when Eve trips over a pile of corpses littered against the side of the church in the center of town. She'd thought the bodies were stairs under the heavy layer of snow and stepped on one in order to take a look inside the building. The collision knocked the snow off one of the faces, and for a deeply horrifying moment, Eve thought it was the face of her mother and turned away, covering her mouth in utter terror before realizing it wasn't her mom. But once she connected the story her father had told her about her parents' last night together and the fact that she knew almost everyone in the town from her own youth, she decided she didn't want to take the chance of (literally) stumbling across anyone she knew. They retreated back to the house and haven't gone on another walk since. The upturned face haunted her dreams thereafter, its single open eye staring accusingly from its wreath of snow, a silent reprimand on its frozen visage.

A couple of nights later, Eve is settling herself under the multiple layers of blankets she requires to sleep comfortably when the doorknob to her room gently turns. For a moment, she's worried it's Ned, who had several straight bourbons that evening and was slurring his words by the time they agreed they were all ready for bed. Clutching her covers to her chin, she watches the door swing slowly open to reveal Amy's much smaller figure in the flickering glow of the candle Eve hasn't blown out yet. "Amy, are you okay?" she asks, concerned by the silence from the child, who hasn't made a sound and is just standing in the doorway.

"Can I sleep in here with you? Please?"

Alarmed that perhaps Ned has tried something, Eve's heart rate accelerates in a combination of anger and fear. They're alone out here, after all. "Did something happen?"

"I … I just wanted to not be alone," the girl says in a quiet voice with a hint of a snuffle.

Relieved, Eve tosses back one side of the blankets and gestures for Amy to come and climb into the bed.

"Thanks," Amy says as she snuggles under the covers and nudges up firmly against Eve's side. "I miss my mom."

Eve's heart weakens at this, both because the poor thing is a foster child to begin with, and because her mother abandoned her for some reason and is certainly dead now if not beforehand. It must be hard for Amy's young mind to wrap itself around such things. Eve slips an arm around her to pull her in closer. "You know what, Amy? I miss mine too. I do. You're okay now though. I'll take care of you."

A mumble from beneath the covers follows, and Eve spends the next hour wide awake, listening to the girl breathe gently next to her, being soothed herself by the warmth of the smaller body and steadiness of Amy's breathing, and thinking about the new reality and everything that comes with it before finally drifting off. For the first time since leaving North Carolina and arriving here to find the barely living remnant of her father, Eve rests deeply, dreaming of a lake other than the one she's near; it's a smaller one, its surface smooth and peaceful.

It's a nice dream.

Part III: Gathering

CHAPTER 7

Spring 2014 ... again

Winter eventually winds down almost as abruptly as it began. One morning simply feels and smells different as Eve and Ned stand on the porch overlooking the frozen lake that stretches out in a uniform silvery white blanket from the clusters of barren trees lining its shores. The humidity has increased, and the early morning sun shines brightly against the alabaster surface, forcing them to squint against the glare. Steam rises from their mugs of instant coffee and drifts in the mild but warmer breeze to dissipate a few inches from the surfaces of the liquid. Eve feels content after the months of forced confinement in the house, having grown ever closer to Amy, and knows she's now viewed as a surrogate mother. Amy asks the endless questions of youth, riddling her about this and that, and Eve is thrilled that she feels so comfortable with her. They've slept in the same bed for quite a while, taking comfort in the other's warmth and presence. Ned has remained on the couch in the family room so he can tend to the fire as needed throughout the nights, and as a group, they've gone through their days in a peaceful routine like a real family who is just happy to have time together.

Ned breaks the silence first, keeping his voice low since Amy continues the heavy slumber that children manage far better than adults. She can sleep for close to twelve hours a night, which is enviable. "Seems like we'll have some clear roads soon," he says. "Once the sun gets strong enough to get to some of the bare spots and reach the blacktop, it'll accelerate the melting, and we could probably drive in about a week."

She nods and then adds, "It will be nice to have a change of location. Even though this is my childhood home, it doesn't feel like home anymore. Not with all the years that have passed and my father dying in his room. It's felt like his spirit was still lurking a little bit in the house, even though the winter's been nice enough with the three of us together. I can't imagine what it would have been like if I'd been alone for all these months."

Ned grins at that, taking the compliment, and leans a bit closer to her as he speaks. "You know, we don't have to go there to join your friends. We don't know if they're still alive or if things have changed or if it would be okay for all of us to go. As bad as the winter is here, it's probably worse up there, and from what you said, their cabin doesn't sound exactly modern and might not handle the cold as well as this house does. We could find another house here, kind of start anew."

He continues on after a pause, as if a thought has just popped into his mind. "And … you said that you and

DeeDee both seemed to be getting close to that guy, but that it was complicated since there were three of you. If it's just been the two of them, maybe something's developed? Would that upset you?"

She's considered that and admits to herself that it would be upsetting since she was the first one he met. She took great solace in how he'd cared for her, protecting her from Jack—and the zombies, of course—and had always been a gentleman to all the women. It's impossible not to be attracted to him for those qualities, plus he's handsome in a rugged, athletic way and has a ridiculous build honed by the requirements of survival. But her hesitancy on that front is outweighed by the thought that if her "new" group joins the "old" group, they'll have a greater measure of safety and company plus another girl for Amy to have for companionship, and she says as much to Ned.

His face flickers to a brief scowl, like someone who's just sipped from their coffee mug and found that the contents are cold, but then he brightens immediately. "That makes sense. A bigger group for safety, company for all of us. I get it. I just thought that we had a nice thing going here, and it seems pretty safe since the cold weather must have wiped a bunch of them out," he replies with a nod of his chin out to the distance. "Just wanted to throw the option of not leaving out there. I've really enjoyed our time together, Eve. I feel close to you, unlike any relationships I've had in the past, and I like moments like this where it's just the two of us."

Some of that leaves Eve a little unsettled since she has not been thinking about Ned like that at all, and the explicit exclusion of Amy is unthinkable in her mind after months of developing that bond. He's nice enough and is pleasant-looking in a very ordinary kind of way, but she's never felt any spark of attraction despite their close quarters and how well they've gotten to know one another over the last few months. She pushes the thoughts away and concentrates on the near future, but she smiles lightly in response without making eye contact. She isn't aware that Ned, however, is watching her carefully and indeed notices that the smile seems forced.

They drift back indoors and revert to discussing the trip, agreeing to begin packing that day. Even though it's only one hundred miles to their destination and shouldn't take long to drive, they decide to stock the truck with enough provisions for a week and, of course, to bring every weapon they can get their hands on out of precaution. This truck is older, so it only has a bench seat in the cab, but the three of them will fit just fine for the two- or three-hour trip. Nothing should be complicated about this, and Eve fishes out the directions from the desk off the kitchen. Ned studies them over her shoulder and comments that it's a simple enough route, one he partly traveled for work back in the day. The only concern is if there's more snow on the dirt roads leading to the final stretch to the house, but since the truck has four-wheel drive, even that won't be an issue unless it's really deep, and not like the heavy, wet stuff now drizzling off the edges of the roof, spattering on the surface of the deck as they speak.

CHAPTER 8

A cross the plains of middle America and on into the eastern foothills of the Rockies, winter's deposits cling tenaciously to the shady sides of hills. But where the sun's rays can penetrate, the spring starts to melt the snow earlier than it does across the eastern part of the country, though only just barely. Morgan awakens one morning, makes her own coffee, and, after bundling a heavy wool blanket around her, steps out onto her deck, smelling and sensing the difference in the atmosphere that signals the beginning of winter's end. The surface of the deck is already mostly clear of snow since she kept shoveling it throughout the winter for something to do as well as for the exercise. She also scrubbed off the blood stains from the initial battle that feels like eons ago.

The forced solitude and isolation of the cold weather months has not been good for her—she's horribly restless and feels unhealthy from the limited time spent outdoors over that time. While she's retained the routines of showering, exercising, and so on, the house *may* have suffered a smidge from neglect for cleaning. Books of all shapes and sizes litter every possible surface like the aftermath of a discount store at the end of Black Friday. She's read hundreds as well as begun dozens of others, but she discards those that don't capture her interest. Life is too short now for frivolous reading.

Like most people, she's taken some of the simple benefits of civilization for granted, especially things like snow plows. The house is built so far up the hillside that even with the off-road ability of the Jeep, she's been unable to get out. Rather, she can get out easily enough, but she knows there's no way she'll be able to get back up in the vehicle, so she has only gone out for snowshoe hikes about once a week. She's ready, *really* ready, to get back outdoors and onto the road to go see if her brother lives. Being trapped in the house makes her understand the complaints of her (few) white-collar friends who told her that the repetitive nature of office work—get up, shower, go to work in the cube, eat lunch at the desk, come home, eat dinner, log back in for extra work on the handy laptop the company thoughtfully provided for just that reason, go to bed, rise, rinse, repeat— makes them feel as if they're literally missing life. In fact, before the end of the world, there had been something about an underground band that was gaining popularity singing about, of all things, the plight of the office worker in modern days. It was a three-person band, two men and one woman, and they had some catchy name that now eludes her. The Minions? Cube Jockeys? Something in that vein.

Admiring the sprawling vista that opens endlessly before her, Morgan notes the absence of clouds, jet streams, and humanity's ambient noise; it's as peaceful a sight as a person could want. Snow's perfect coating stretches to the horizon, with only evergreens and other trees jutting out of the otherwise pristine surface. She suddenly loathes the emptiness of the view, seeing it as a symbol of her confinement, and makes her own decision to start packing and preparing for her trip. The Jeep isn't going to be what she drives. Oh no. Something much faster and wilder is going to be required to help her shake the winter doldrums, but she'll drive the Jeep down the hill to go car shopping. One or two more days.

Those days pass in preparation, gathering the limited supplies she thinks will be right for what should be just a few days on the road—maybe four, at worst, if there are wrecks she needs to work around or poor weather on the way. Clothes, blankets for sleeping in the car—whatever it turns out to be—the Bo, machete, shotgun and handgun for weapons, and water and food. The forced diet of the present makes her miserable; she'd been a serious foodie before everything went to hell and insisted on all her food being as fresh as it could be. Eating out of cans and packages infuriates her, and while she appreciates the preservatives in the food that keep it edible, she can't stand looking at the labels to see what she's putting in her body. She hopes she'll eventually be able to settle somewhere near farmland that can provide at least some measure of fresh vegetables. Even if her brother isn't there, Upstate New York will work; it has corn—one of her favorites and a broadly planted crop—not to mention other typical summer vegetables and many varieties of berries on the wild shrubs all over the lake area.

She heads across 74 East until it runs into Route 8, heading for a Chevrolet dealership just south of Lakewood. One of her golfing acquaintances worked there as a detailer, and while he'd been lukewarm about all the current models, he raved about the Corvette, so she thinks she'll start there. There's one of everything in Denver, but she's crossed most of the exotic cars off her mental list almost immediately, deciding that if she's going to take a road trip, it's going to be in an American muscle car. If there's anything that reflects the American spirit better than one of those muscle cars, Morgan doesn't know what it could be. The crop of Mustangs, Camaros, Challengers, and Corvettes—arguably not a muscle car, but it's very American, and anything with a V8 and stick shift counts in her book—all retain a measure of the loud, fast, garishly painted and amazingly styled heritage and visceral thrill of their predecessors from the 1960s and early 1970s. All of them will snort to life with the bravado of a star quarterback before a big game and travel well across the country, so now it's just a matter of taste.

It takes her two minutes from when she pulls into the lot, if that. Sitting out front of the dealership, on display like a supermodel preening before a Parisian crowd, is *the* car. Red paint and sharp angles everywhere, with scoops, vents, and glorious body panels stretching across massive wheels and tires; the whole package looks like it wants to explode into motion and devour the asphalt between here and New York in minutes, not hours. She turns off the Jeep and hops out, leaving the door open, and stalks around the gleaming car, admiring its unique combination of beauty and aggression—and perhaps making a small note that it's a perfect reflection of herself—and deciding on the spot that she's done shopping.

The car and dealership are locked, so she makes her own key by tossing a wooden and wrought iron bench seat through the broad panes of glass in the showroom. After the glittering shower subsides, she steps over the threshold and finds the cabinet containing all the key fobs for their inventory. She then realizes she hasn't made note of the stock number of the Corvette, so she just grabs all the keys on the row labeled Vettes and walks back outside.

Shit.

The noise from either her Jeep arriving or the glass explosion has brought out the security team, though this one isn't armed with mace and a flashlight, and the odds are definitely not in her favor since all her weapons are sitting in the passenger seat of the Jeep. A baker's dozen of the monsters loom across the parking lot, mixed in among the cars, trucks, and SUVs, all of them marching relentlessly toward her as she stands just outside the building. The pack is a blend of males and females and, sadly, two child zombies who couldn't have been older than preteens when they were turned. The zombies exhibit varied levels of decay, some looking like they must have been among the originals. They're beginning to look tired and worn out—skin graying ever more steadily, teeth missing from yawning mouths that open and close reflexively in hunger as they approach, and clothes fraying beyond even what a homeless person would discard. Morgan gets the sense they can't last forever.

Maybe they'll eventually run down like batteries, but one of them looks pretty damn fresh and clean, wearing what looks like running gear, all the way down to a reflective neon yellow vest.

Zombie, Tahoe, zombie, Camaro, zombie, Impala, zombie.

Jesus, it's like shopping for cars in the old days. And the most dangerous thing she has on her is a pocketknife with a whopping three-inch blade. Super.

Muuuuuuuhhhhh!

Without hesitation, Morgan turns left and darts across the lot, furious with herself for the lapse in awareness. The months of slaughtering zombies with abandon have made her a bit dismissive of the threat they pose, but without weapons, she's at a huge disadvantage. Her speed and endurance—they're what she's going to rely on now, and luckily, she doesn't own a single pair of shoes that aren't good for running; she goes at a fast trot so the horde can follow her visually. She's learned during her many hunts that if you run away too quickly, they lose interest after a few hundred yards and simply stop and mill around aimlessly until something else catches their interest. Today, she wants to keep them tracking her for a good half mile or more. That way, she can then circle back at a sprint and take off before they return (if at all) or at least reach her weapons and balance things out a bit if they do.

Without looking back, she jogs down the road, hearing the uneven scuffle of the many pairs of feet in pursuit. After going several blocks, she pauses and turns to face them, counting heads to see if there are going to be any surprises when she leads them down some side streets before losing them and going back to the Jeep. A dozen heads bob as they do the awkward zombie jog after her, and when they see her stop, they increase their own speed in anticipation of victory … and lunch.

The one dressed for a jog is gone. Hmm ….

She scans all directions to see if perhaps he was smart enough to take a parallel street in an attempt to flank her, but there's nothing in sight other than those right here on the main drag. A bit unnerving, but first things first. She yells, "Hey!" at the pack and breaks off to the nearest side street, her running shoes pounding the pavement more quickly now as she ups her speed and goes three more blocks, turns right, goes right again at the end of the next building, comes back to the original street, and turns right again. All clear, so she jogs back to the dealership lot.

There he is.

The jogger.

He's just standing there between her and the open door of the Jeep, facing her as if he knew all along what she was going to do. A wild mess of curly blonde hair hangs heavily over his forehead, obscuring his left eye and cheek. He's wearing fairly new running shoes, shorts, and a compression shirt, so he must be a *really* new zombie. She wonders if he was like her, holed up for the crappy weather and, once spring broke, decided to do something normal after being cooped up but then ran—*Oh … ha … I see what you did there*—into trouble. Morgan digs into the pocket of her cargo shorts for the knife, such as it is, just to have something.

No knife.

It must have fallen out when she was running away from the group. *Wonderful*, she thinks, *just me and him, bare hands unless I can get to the Jeep.* The zombie's at least fifty pounds larger than she is, with the muscular build of a football player more than a runner's slender build. Bulky through the shoulders and upper chest, slim in the waist before thickening at the hips and legs, which are heavily muscled as well. He definitely looks like someone who has spent a ton of time outdoors and in the gym like her. While she would have spent time admiring him in other circumstances, she's going to need to figure out a way to kill him.

She circles a few steps to the left, and he tracks her with his visible eye and pivots just slightly so he remains facing her. Then she continues around to the far side of the Jeep and the closed passenger door. Figuring she's quick enough to dart in, open the door, and grab something before he gets to her, she's nonplussed to watch him walk almost casually around it to keep her away from the vehicle. Morgan completes the circuit, as does her antagonist, and stops, frustrated and aware that the other dozen of them may well be on their way back here within the next couple of minutes. The route she led them on is no more than a half mile away, so at their normal pace, she has maybe six or seven minutes before they return, and she's just pissed away at least two of those minutes with the walk-around.

Dive under the car? She could fit, but it wouldn't be quick, not with the way he's moving—gracefully and … with confidence. Is he more intelligent than the others? The terrifying thought that some of them may not be slow, single-minded killing machines clamps onto her consciousness like the assault of a mountain lion on a foolish toy dog. She needs to end this, now, but has no clear idea of how to do so other than hand to hand. That's the one method she hasn't experimented with in her studies—no way is she going to get close enough to one of them, whose rage fuels a strength she can't compete with equally.

Nope, no need to fight fair with them at all, but now she's forced to. As she steps forward and settles into a hybrid martial arts stance borne of her varied training, she hears a not-so-faint ....

Muuuuuuuhhhhh!

They're coming, and her opponent doesn't budge, clearly knowing she wants to get to the vehicle and not letting her do so.

Fine.

Lunging forward, she strikes with her right foot, hitting the inside of his right knee with a savage blow. No snap like she'd hoped, but he still staggers. Yet he instantly stands back upright and leers at her, almost like he's saying, "Is that the best you've got?"

Actually, no.

This time she attacks in a blur, driving her left foot into his groin—not even a grunt—her right foot into the has-to-be-damaged knee again—deeper stagger this time; a mashed joint is a mashed joint, after all—and then strikes the side of his head with her right elbow. There's a ferocious *crack* when the jaw breaks and some of his teeth are scattered onto the pavement. Not allowing him a moment to recover or retaliate, she drives her left hand up into his nose, missing the killing blow she intended but still smashing it in a spectacular way and bringing forth a spray of blood that splatters across his face and vest. The monster reels back, unsteady on his feet with the shattered knee joint and the series of blows, and she completes the assault by sweeping the bad leg once more to knock it down. More blood as his head bounces off the ebony asphalt of the freshly paved parking lot, and she flips him over quickly while he's stunned, not sure if she can do what she has in mind but determined to try. Despite her strength, without a weapon, there isn't an easy way to kill another human, not for someone her size.

With a glance back to the street, she sees a handful of the other zombies emerging around the corner of a building several blocks away, perhaps four hundred yards. She drops to her knees on the zombie's back, her weight pinning it, and reaches around to grasp its chin in both hands, cupping it in her palms. Straining with every ounce of power she has, she pulls up, up, up, tilting the back of the monster's head ever so steadily toward his own back. The big muscles of her upper back and shoulders quiver with the effort, and she switches positions to keep one knee on the spine and the other leg braced down against the road, pushing and pulling for all she's worth. She doesn't think she can do it and feels the zombie stir beneath her, his broken jaw straining against the pressure of her hands, seeking to open and bite her. Redoubling her efforts, she arches her back and *pulls*, finally feeling something give at the same time as a

nauseating *snap* sounds, and the head in her hands suddenly becomes dead weight.

There's no time to spare. She drops the head and leaps for the Jeep and her weapons. She knows she could take off, but she's inflamed by the fight and dead set on winning here as well as acquiring the Corvette. Two shotguns, one loaded with slugs and one with shot, the Glock she found in a neighbor's house, and the machete all come out to play. Settling her breathing from the effort she's just expended, she rests the loaded shotgun across the hood of the Jeep and begins firing at the five zombies that are now within fifty yards and closing. The first one stumbles to a halt and tips over two steps after its head vanishes in a scarlet mist; the second doesn't realize it's down to one leg for a moment and then totters to the ground before crawling onward, its fingernails shredding against the tarmac as it tries to pull itself along. Morgan exchanges shotguns for the close-in work and finishes off the last three—*Bang! Bang! Bang!*—decorating the street with sprays of viscera and random bits and pieces as the shots tear and shred and end the fight. No other zombies come into view, and she finally expels the breath she didn't realize she'd been holding.

Muuuuuuuhhhhh ....

This one is a faint, sad groan more than a battle cry. It comes from the one whose neck she broke, and she's horrified to see him struggle to his feet like a drunk—a nightmare drunk whose head is tipped impossibly backward. All she can see is his Adam's apple and the tip of his nose atop the neck, but the goddamn abomination is still trying to come and get her. Fighting back the gorge rising in her throat, Morgan sets the second shotgun down on the hood of the Jeep, chambers a round in the Glock, and fires into the bobbing mass of flesh. The bullet goes through the legacy of the first man and carries through to the roof of the skull, finally finishing the job. He drops down heavily to the asphalt, unmoving.

Shuddering from the vision and the conflict, Morgan stills her breathing as quickly as she can and begins to transfer her supplies over to the Corvette. The Bo is an awkward fit at first since there's no back seat, but it works fine between the front seats and extending back into the luggage space. Part of her is tempted to remove the roof panel, but since there are another seven zombies unaccounted for, she decides against it.

Luckily, the car is keyless, so she doesn't have to figure out which of the handful of key fobs she's grabbed from inside is for this one; she just jabs the clutch and then the start button. Eight wonderful cylinders spark and sing to life, idling with the grace of a ballerina … one that can tear your head off. It's been a while since she's driven a stick shift, but she keeps it simple and revs the engine, dumps the clutch, and leaves the lot in a cloud of smoke, trailing twin ebony streaks of burned rubber out onto the road.

After dodging the bodies of the fallen zombies littering the street, she accelerates through the gears and heads for the nearest entrance to I-70 East. Her Colorado chapter is over, but she's going to take the image of the smart, strategic zombie with her on the trip east, the way a song from your youth pops on the radio, brings forth the memories tied to that song, that time, and haunts the you of now, for better or worse.

***

Exiting the city—not too quickly, thanks to a generous scattering of maybe abandoned cars here and there on the highway winding through it—Morgan breaks loose of the eastern suburbs and stares through the slanted windshield at the beginning of the plains that are going to dominate her view for the next couple of days. Tired from the fight over the Corvette and from the flood and retraction of adrenaline, she finds herself idly wishing for a drive-through coffee house on her route to perk her up. Not a serious coffee drinker, she nevertheless takes issue with the homogenization of the drink over the past decade. She has a whole host of soap boxes and takes issue with many things, but this is one of the largest—aside from the jarring fascination with celebrities or people famous for being famous, which makes no sense. If you want coffee, you go to Starbucks; Italian food, you go to Carrabba's or Olive Garden; tools, off to Home Depot or Lowe's; and you'd drive your generic car or SUV that looked like all the others. Going, going, now gone are the days of the wonderful American ingenuity, independence, can-do attitude, and uniqueness that made it a great country in the earlier days, only to then be covered over by sprawling malls and shopping enclaves where everything was all the same, everywhere. In the past, Morgan avoided each of the chains over the years, eschewing them for the ever-dwindling alternatives where she could get to know the staff—or, *gasp*, the owner—over the course of months and try new things rather than accept that the ubiquitous chains were the best. Today, though, she would gladly drive through a Dunkin', as she's uncomfortably exhausted and resolves to only drive until dark so she can see what she's doing. Cracking the window to allow the bracing spring air serve as a surrogate for caffeine, Morgan also cracks a grin and pushes hard on the gas pedal.

After spending some of her early drive sprinting the car to well over 100 miles per hour and getting a feel for it— now this, *this* is still something properly American; nothing else like a Corvette anywhere—she settles into the habit of life before zombies and drifts subconsciously back down near the speed limit for a few hours as the shadow of her red bullet lengthens in the dwindling light of the afternoon while the day runs out of steam. One fuel stop along the way is all she needs since the dealership had thankfully filled the tank, and she's been able to gather gas from lawn mower cans across a handful of houses in a nameless town off one of the few exits. Her resolution to sleep in the car made sense, but after pulling into a rest stop—again, out of habit—and seeing a handful of cars spotted throughout the lot, she realizes it will be safer if she's in the middle of nowhere and pulls right back out. Another thirty minutes has her indeed in the middle of Nowhere, Kansas—not a real place, but a few hundred miles into the eastern part of the state—and with absolutely nothing in sight other than fields that are going to rest untended for the foreseeable future, she slips the car into neutral and lets it coast to a stop on the shoulder.

She takes a few minutes to relieve herself by the side of the road, unworried about dangling her caboose in the breeze and happy she thought at the last minute before leaving home to bring a handful of rolls of toilet paper. The night falls quickly as she sits on the hood of the car, munching a granola bar and polishing off a few bottles of water while watching the horizon in all distances to confirm nothing is in sight that could threaten her. Satisfied by the time the world goes full dark, Morgan slumps into the passenger seat so she won't have to deal with the steering wheel, and after cracking the driver's side window for fresh air, checking that the car is locked, and wrapping herself snugly, she drifts quickly to sleep.

***

She awakes with a start.

It's early, *very* early, with the sun not quite over the horizon in front of her but tentatively throwing its rays against the edge of the world to cast some sparse light on the road ahead. Something has triggered her to wake up; feeling uneasy, she sits up and looks quickly around the car for a horde of zombies closing in. There are none, and for a moment, she begins to succumb to the wispy tendrils of sleep pulling her back under the blanket and into the cushioned depths of the car seat, but then she sits back upright, now fully awake.

There's something out there. A figure far, far up the road, marching right down the center of the blacktop, swinging its arms in wild patterns. A person? A monster? Whatever it is, it's backlit by the scant illumination and shadowed from the front, as if painted deep ebony, and still too far away for her to make out clearly.

And then she suddenly and desperately needs to pee. As in, right now, she has a miserably full bladder, and she remembers she drank two full bottles of water the previous night before falling asleep and swears silently at herself.

Oh, for crying out loud.

Not like she could've forecasted a morning visitor, but she's still aggravated since she seriously needs to go, and there's no way she's going to take her eyes off the growing walker who's steadily making its way west on I-70. Drawing the shotgun out with her and leaning it against the scarlet paint of the car's rear quarter panel, she simply drops her drawers at the side of the pavement and does her business while watching the character, who's still swinging its right arm in patterns across its body. She finally catches the shimmer of something silver in one of the passes.

A weapon, likely a sword.

A weapon means an actual person since the zombies haven't been inclined to carry anything so far, but that still isn't necessarily a good thing. An armed human has just as much potential for a bad outcome as a zombie, maybe even more since a zombie will quickly get to the point and kill you while a person has the unlimited capacity for inflicting misery on their fellow man or woman. All the survivors, the few she's come across anyway, fall into one of two categories: individuals or very small groups who scavenge and remain hidden as much as possible and only come out for supplies when needed but run away if they come across anyone else, and the pack hounds who typically rove in groups of at least ten members of mixed genders, all armed to the teeth and indiscriminate about whether they are killing zombies or humans. She has chased a few of the former, trying to speak with them, but they rapidly scurried away when they saw her and disappeared into warrens of hiding places in the city. She's avoided the latter groups after observing what they are capable of—nothing pleasant for anyone they came across, zombie or human. Both groups always have weapons—this far past Z-Day, you're armed or you're dead.

So in theory, this is going to be one of the scavenger types, which implies less aggressive and less likely to try and kill or hurt her. Okay, that means she'll carefully wait to see if she can talk to this one versus driving past them and continuing on the rest of her journey.

From what she can see, the silhouette steadily covers the ground between them and seems taller than average, so she guesses this is a man. Since they're traveling in opposite directions, she could stand to hear some news, if there is any, of what faces her in the east, especially since she's nearing Kansas City soon and will avoid the city if it's overrun with danger. Leaning a hip against the car, she holds the shotgun lightly, pointed down (for now), and just watches.

Early morning silence reigns. This is the middle of nowhere, after all, and few have lived here to begin with. Of those, all are now gone. No birds are singing since there are no trees in sight for them to rest or nest in. Just her, the car, and the shimmer of a man in the distance coming closer but far enough away that she can't hear his footsteps yet.

After a minute or two longer, the figure checks its pace for a moment, just a brief interruption in what has been a steady walk, and she knows he's seen her. The swordplay, for that's indeed what it is, stops as the man sheathes it and resumes walking toward her at a quicker pace than before.

More waiting ... and then he stops a dozen paces away from her, dusty cowboy boots scuffing the yellow center line as he halts. Tall is right, somewhere around six-foot-four, and skinny. Almost everyone is skinnier now, of course. But his clothes fit just fine even though they're obviously well-worn, so he must have stayed skinny all along. A shock of dreadlocked hair goes off in every direction, like an insane person's angry drawing, carrying well down past his shoulders; the dreadlocks are mostly brown with scraps of what look like ribbon, tinsel, and feathers threaded into the ends and fixed with hair ties. A hat. A pirate hat. Not quite the giant cartoonish swashbuckler type but pretty damn close. The sword hangs in a dark scabbard belted through blue jeans that are worn and a bit grimy, hanging over his bony hips. He's wearing a lightweight, brown jacket over a white T-shirt with slashes of neon green writing across it, angled up toward his left shoulder. The top line reads, "RENC," and the second reads, "ONKE."

It takes her a minute, and then she recalls the underground band she struggled to bring to mind before.

Trench Monkeys, that's it. All three band members had been within shouting distance of forty on one side or the other, and they were a hysterical mix: part dark parody of the white-collar-office world and part solid punk and metal vibe. Simple yet compelling. Songs like "Come Into My Cube, There's Almost Room for Two," "Turkey Sandwich for Lunch Again," and "I Can See the Future and It Looks the Same as the Present" from their debut album, *Is It Friday Yet?* crept onto Pandora and other online channels as they struck a chord with their peers. Right after they'd gone wildly viral, everything came to a screeching halt, thanks to the zombies. Shame. Their music was great, and their band name was really catchy too.

A wispy beard, all curly and wild with two braided handlebars drooping over the outer edges of a surprisingly kind mouth, smudges across the man's face and neck. For the getup, she'd have expected someone who fashioned himself a tough guy, but as she studies his face further, especially his eyes, she sees not a shred of malice. Instead, there's perhaps a touch of simplicity, a mild innocence to his face, but she's going to keep space between them nonetheless.

He speaks first, and she isn't really surprised that his deep voice just happens to speak in a patois of pirate and Jamaican, though he's as white as the snow-draped Colorado mountains she left behind the day before. "Ahoy there! Ye be a fine bonnie lass, drivin' a fine bonnie chariot. Who are ye and where is it ye be headin', missie? You won't be havin' any need for yon boom stick what you got in your hand there."

A pirate.

She's in the middle of the country in the throes of the zombie apocalypse, and she meets a guy walking down the highway who dresses, talks, and acts like a fucking pirate. You can't make this stuff up. But he seems harmless despite the sword, and after all, she *does* have the "boom stick," which means if he pulls anything, she'll blow him to messy pieces across the eastern lanes of the highway, so there's no risk in seeing where this goes. "I'm Morgan. I'm going east to New York," she replies while pointing down the road behind him. "Where are you going?"

His face darkens, and she tightens her grip on the shotgun, tipping the barrel up a hair in his direction. "East, the way from where the sun comes," he says heavily. "But the bad place is back dat way. He say it's a sank-churry, but it's no such place. Shiver me timbers!" Lord, he actually said it. "You dinna want to be going dere, no, Missie Morgan. There be no happy times in de houses with more walls place." His eyebrows sit thick over his eyes as he says this, clearly bothered, but she can't understand what he means.

"Sank-churry? What's that?"

"They say it's a sank-churry, but it ain't. None of them be safe there, 'specially those of woman type. Forced me to leave, they did after I stopped 'em." He becomes agitated, a tear rolling out of one eye to vanish into the thicket of his beard, and his hand picks at the edge of his jacket in a fluttering pattern.

Morgan can't translate the words. They don't make sense to her at all, but whatever this "sank-churry" is, it obviously isn't on the tourist maps. She wants to settle him down and maybe change the subject—while he may appear to be a mad Jamaican pirate without a mean bone in his body, the topic is obviously upsetting, and she just isn't up to killing a person unless she needs to. So she works to cool him down. "You know what? I just woke up and I'm hungry. You look hungry too. Do you want to have some breakfast with me? Some water too? I have plenty in my chariot," she says with a gentle grin. No fool, she walks around the far side of the car to keep it between them, opens the passenger door, and brings out a box of protein granola bars and two large bottles of water. Retracing her steps back to the middle of the road, she sits down and pulls the box open.

"Aye! I kin have some of those victuals if ye please. It ha' been a day or two or more since I had any food, and I be true starvin'." He plops merrily down on the road, the gloom vanishing from his visage as he does so.

Food and men, she thinks. *So predictable.*

She takes one of the bars for herself and passes him the box, which he digs into quickly, devouring two bars before she's scarcely nibbled her first. "Thank ye, Morgan. I do thank ye."

"Keep the whole thing. I have more in the car." A big smile from him, and she gets the sense that kindness is something he's received in small measure in the past.

They sit in comfortable silence for a few moments, munching and drinking, but then they eventually begin to talk more. He tells her he's heading west since he's always wanted to see the mountains of Colorado, and he figures the colder weather will cut down on "them silent people beasties."

At first, she thinks about discouraging him from going there because she's pondering if he'll be good company heading east, not to mention she thinks maybe someone needs to look after him. But as if reading her mind, he tells her there's no way he'll skip the trip to see the mountains now he's free. Disappointed, she tells him she's lived there and describes how he can find her house if he likes; she doesn't need it anymore, and since it's fairly self-sustaining, he'll have it easy there. This brings a huge grin to his face and more thanks. It doesn't take her long to confirm he's mildly impaired, all there but not terribly deep beyond the simple things. He pays no attention to how she looks, which is a rarity, especially given she's in a very snug camisole and short shorts, all of her pretty much on display. His lack of awareness confirming he isn't on the same wavelength as your typical man. She asks him where he came from before.

"Oh, aye. I been at the 'ospital for long years. You ken see I'm maybe a wee bit off, but there be no danger to others bein' near me, unless there's someone be troubling a lass. Then it all goes dark like in my head till a wee bit later, and it's always been a mess while 'twas dark." The scowl is back as he remembers his blackouts. "When the monsters came through the 'ospital and killed an' ate the others, I got out an' away. Went to dere place with de walls and guns, I did, which was okay till he did what he did and I had to leave. Weren't no way to be treatin' a girlie."

Morgan doesn't like the sound of this "bad place" and is going a bit nuts trying to decipher what it really is due to his accent and manner of speaking, but she asks him how to find it since she's still going that way.

He frowns. "Ye canna miss it. There be signs all over the highway from bot' ways. I left three days ago," he says while only holding up two fingers. "Dere be some miles 'tween here and dere, but your car will eat 'em up fast enough I t'ink. Girlies shouldna be goin dere though. Especial ones who're pretty like nice Missie Morgan. Him, he likes de pretty ones. It's no a good place for ye. Dinna go!" Another tear drips down his cheek and actually vanishes into his moustache this time.

Morgan's normally hardened heart aches a bit for this soft, simple soul and whatever happened to him in this mystery place. She isn't sure whether she'll see the signs he's talking about, and if she does, she'll check the place out, but she just reassures him she'll stay away. What he's said about things happening to women has her full attention; she seethes at the idea that someone is abusing women now instead of focusing on staying alive and maybe defeating the zombies somehow and starting over with the world scoured clean. Yeah, now that she thinks about it, there's a good chance she's going to go find "sank-churry" and maybe get into a smidge of a fight if what he's saying has even a hint of truth to it.

Abruptly, the picnic comes to an end when he stands up and announces that it's time for him to be going down the road. Morgan is disappointed and a little sad to see him go;

there's a clean, unspoiled happiness underneath the goofy outfit and speech that reminds her of a child. She's worried he'll simply forget to forage along his trip, so she takes the food and water supplies out of her car, stuffing them into a backpack she can easily replace at the next town. He, however, has about four hundred miles to go, which is going to take him a while, so she reminds him to stop for food and water. He promises he will.

She cleans up after them—not a litterbug, even now—and tosses the trash into the back of the Corvette and fires it up, rippling the ground in gentle tremors she can feel when she steps over to say goodbye.

"Morgan of the red car and pretty face, dinna be goin' to the bad place. Go an' find yer brother in your 'appy place from when ye were but a young'un. It be a bad place, and he be a bad man though he doesna always seem that way. You shouldna go dere, just keep on wit' de drivin'." The shroud of shadow is back on his face as he says this. Then, of all things to do, he suddenly grins and winks at her as he turns and sets his boots upon the road. He unsheathes the sword and begins swinging it across his body in the series of patterns she saw him do before.

And then he's gone.

It isn't until she settles into the car seat and engages the clutch that Morgan realizes she never got his name.

***

The car sings its happy tune as she drives east, pondering her encounter with the pirate and what he meant by "the sank-churry." She knows it's his accent throwing the word into a jumble in her ears, but she can't relax her mental barriers enough to let the answer come to her.

One of her few concessions to spending time with other people used to be a women's support group at a local church. It was not specifically for abused women, though they made up the largest share. It was just women being there for women, a safe place where they could freely talk to strangers about the intensely personal issues they each faced. For the young ones, the pressure to be hot; for those with young children, the loss of self-identity and a shrunken connection with their spouse; for those in their late thirties, early forties, and beyond, the difficulty in maintaining their looks in a society that worshiped youth and vitality; for those with newly retired spouses, the disruption of their space, schedule, and happiness. No one shared their name, just their stories. There were many tears shed in those meetings, many hugs shared; none of those by the strong-willed, silent woman who watched it all. She'd been a listener only, a wraith tucked into the shadows of the hall where the group met, riveted by the complexity of the other women's lives, feeling empathy for those who had lost a child or spouse and rage when anyone reported abuse. Those were the ones she followed home, inconspicuously, and noted where they lived. From time to time, she would swing by their houses looking for an opportunity to catch him solo, such as the husband going out alone or the wife leaving the house. When that happened, she would approach the husband and go about her business in one of several ways. Strike up a conversation with him, flirt, show off some skin, and agree to drinks and more flirting. She'd found that abusers were also usually cheaters, and given her looks, it was too easy to compromise them into going to a hotel, getting them undressed, and then snapping photos of the intended affair. She'd leave—sometimes it took some wrestling, but her martial arts background and willingness to hit first and talk second generally worked well since hitters never liked being hit—and then have the photos printed and sent to the husband's work, home, wife's lawyer's office, and anywhere else she could think of. Her tactic wasn't foolproof, of course, since some victims still wouldn't leave, but she felt that if she could help free some women, it would be her small contribution.

Morgan is no heroine, but she also isn't content to let wrongs go, so she's going to find this "sank-churry" and see what's happening there. It doesn't take long at 100 miles per hour to cover the distance the pirate covered on foot over three (or two) days, and the translation makes her smile with chagrin.

As she closes in on the suburban outlying spaces of Kansas City, she begins to see exit signs listing the food and lodging offerings ahead. However, spray-painted over the first sign in a dense black scrawl is written SAFETY→. The same word is written on another exit, another sign, and then, at the third exit, it changes to SAFETY here, and she lets the Corvette slow and drift off onto the exit ramp. More signs guide her with a black S→ for a mile or so off the highway, and then the oddest structure she's ever seen appears at the outer reach of her vision.

Wishing for a pair of binoculars—*or a telescope; I bet the pirate had a telescope*, she thinks—she edges the car to the curb and turns it off. The place is huge; not tall but wide, but she isn't able to see it clearly enough at this distance for it to make sense to her eyes. Gray sections turn to yellow turn to gray turn to blue turn to gray and so on. She grabs the assortment of key fobs she tossed into the car back at the dealership, steps out of the car, and clicks lock buttons on each until one works. The rest she tosses onto a nearby lawn and then sets off one street to the side so she can scout the building without being seen. Jogging lightly down the road, dodging the occasional abandoned bicycle or car with doors open in the street, she closes in and peers around the corner of a house for a look.

A madman must have dreamt it up, and she briefly thinks the pirate may have made this outrageous construct before dismissing the notion as the scope of it comes into clearer focus. It's a fort—there's no better word for it—right smack in the middle of suburbia. Two-story, modern houses built on small lots no more than a fifth of an acre are joined by cinder-block walls stretching from grass to gutters to both connect the homes and provide a barrier. All the windows on the ground floors are covered from the outside in heavy plywood that's neatly placed and obviously screwed to the siding of the houses or perhaps even bolted through the walls so it can't be removed by bare hands. Platforms at the top are clearly built on the inside of the walls, as she can see indistinct heads and shoulders—lookouts—between houses, which makes her glad she's come forward carefully. From this side, she counts six houses in the outer wall, and in the very middle, between two of the homes, stands a city bus. No ordinary city bus, but one with what looks like a steel skirt fastened to the lower body panels, blocking the space beneath, and heavy bars across the window glass. It blocks a gap in the cinder blocks, so it obviously serves as a roll-aside door to the compound. "SAFETY" is painted high on the gray blocks in large letters. The handwriting looks like someone leaned over the wall to do the writing upside down. Fascinated, Morgan stands and takes it all in for a few minutes, noting the number of guards. There are also some women working outside the walls, dragging something to the side.

Curiosity has gotten her in plenty of trouble over the years, but she's also managed to escape most of those times with nary more than a scrape, so she jogs back, shrugs on a flannel shirt over the camisole, fires up the car, and rolls slowly down the road until she's in sight of the guards, who wave their arms and shout to others behind the walls. The clutch of women at ground level stop what they're doing— the things they're dragging are bodies of zombies—and look at her with their own curiosity as she brings the car to a stop and then executes a K-turn so it's pointed back the way she came. The pirate's ominous warnings and scowls are foremost in her mind, so she isn't going to take any chances. Shutting down the motor, she exits the car and turns around to face the madcap building.

The rumble-rattle of the diesel motor of the bus starts, and the bus rolls back to open a space no more than six feet wide, from which a throng of some twenty or more people emerge. They are led by a tall, blonde man somewhere around forty years old. All of them are dressed in blue denim from head to ankle, all wear dark boots, and all the men in the group are armed in some form or another. She's glad for the Glock tucked in her waistband at her back and covered by the flannel shirt. The leader has a red bandana wrapped around his right arm, has an athlete's build and fluid movement, and is *handsome*. Very, disarmingly handsome. He smiles, displaying magnificent teeth that are as white as if he just departed the dentist's chair. The crowd stops, shuffling to a halt—*almost like the zombie packs*, she thinks—and he continues until he gets closer to her and extends his arms to the sides in a welcoming gesture. His blue eyes flicker over her in an appraising gaze, showing nothing other than pleasure at greeting a guest, but her radar is way, *way* up. Two men stop about halfway between the rest of the crowd and the leader, clearly bodyguards of a sort with black bandanas on their arms and baseball caps pulled low over their eyes. Midwestern muscles bulge from their too-tight shirts. They try to look nonthreatening by keeping their hands away from the pistols in their shoulder harnesses, though they don't exactly pull it off. They're huge men, the type other men keep handy for dirty work.

One of them is holding an enormous German shepherd on a chain, and while everyone else waits, he marches forward with the dog. "Don't move. He's gonna check you

out. Any funny moves, and I'm lettin' him rip you to shreds,"
he snarls, suspicion writ strong on his face.

Morgan sees no need for a reply and holds still while
he walks the dog around her. The dog shows little interest
in her after a casual sniff at her sneakers and then sits at
her feet, gazing up with content caramel eyes. Sensing no
danger, she reaches out a hand to pat his knobby head and
is rewarded with a happy lick from his fat, rough tongue.
Some guard dog.

The handler, obviously nonplussed, drops his end of
the chain and steps back as the leader moves forward.
"Welcome!" he calls out in a clear, powerful voice, loud
enough for the crowd to hear as well. "All are welcome and
can find safety and sanctuary here! I'm Marcus, and these
are my friends."

A strong, compelling voice that's used to command.
The smile adorning his strong features doesn't budge, but
she also notices that it doesn't quite touch the eyes atop the
tanned cheekbones below them. His blonde hair is clean,
and the part of it that isn't pulled back in a man bun drops
to his shoulders. Morgan would have been thrilled if the
fashion horror of the man bun had died along with most
of the rest of the bad habits of humanity, but he pulls it off
okay. "Nice …," he says slowly as his eyes drizzle languidly
down and then back up her figure with a scant glance over
her shoulder, "car." A small smirk at his own joke. "What's
your name?"

At first, she hesitates to introduce herself, feeling as if
giving her name means surrendering something, some

measure of power, but these are people, a bunch of them. The first group she's seen still surviving and apparently living safely behind their towering walls of cement. She scans the homogenously dressed crowd and sees a little of everything—men and women in roughly equal proportion, a scattering of children and teens, but no one older than about fifty. Most of the survivors she saw in Colorado had been young as well, but there had been some measure of every age. She wonders if there's any significance to it here.

"Hello there? Are you okay? Can you speak?" He interrupts her reverie and brings her back to the moment, and when she focuses on his face again, she sees he's still smiling a game-show-host smile. He has the natural charisma that all good-looking people have, but more on top of that as well.

"Morgan. My name is Morgan."

"Morgan! What a pretty name for such a beautiful woman. Perfect! Welcome again. We're glad you found us. Did you follow the signs?"

"Yes, though I was told to look for them by someone. Otherwise, I might have driven right past them."

At this, his features cloud over briefly, clearly trying to figure out who she met and told her about the signs. "Who might that have been? We count our people every morning and evening, just making sure no one is outside the walls before dark falls as we button down for the nights. You know why, of course."

Morgan watches him watching her, not comfortable with the scrutiny as he mentally wrestles with whom her informant was. She also wonders about the "why" in his statement and whether it's about the safety of his flock or something else.

Again hesitating to share more than she needs to, she makes the decision to hedge a bit just in case. "It was a tall guy dressed as a pirate, talked like a pirate. Nice as can be but maybe not quite all there. He didn't tell me his name though. You must know him?"

"Jack! You met Captain Jack, or such as he styles himself. He's buggier than a Louisiana swamp in the summertime, and those movies took him over the edge into 'I'm Captain Jack Sparrow-land.' Thank goodness he doesn't do all of that waving-his-hands-around nonsense, but he is a harmless fellow. We should go collect him so he's not out there alone and in danger. We've been wondering where he'd gotten off to. I'll send some of the boys to go pick him up. Which direction did you say you came from?"

"I didn't," she says with the challenge in her voice kept subtle. She doesn't trust Marcus or his "boys" to do anything other than maybe run down Captain Jack where he walks or, maybe worse given how he's talked about it, bring him back to a place that has made him miserable. This is going nowhere; she doesn't need anything from these people since she can resupply anywhere else, and her drive will only take a day or two more anyway. This place has the stink of something other than sanctuary, but these are people, and not all survivors can be bad apples, so she decides to stay for a little bit and learn more.

"I see," he says, a flicker of annoyance across his face. "So I can tell from the look on your face that he must have told you about the little misunderstanding a few days ago. He went out with one of the work details later that day and must have wandered off. That poor bugger's muddled mind reads everything in black and white, and he was upset that day when we imposed discipline on one of the others. Discipline is our most important rule for survival, you know. If we all follow the rules all the time, we all stay alive.

"We had to punish one of our members, an expulsion, and it was someone who had connected with Jack and watched out for him a bit. We prefer for all to pull their own weight since that's how we remain safe and how everyone contributes to our little society. But despite Jack's less-than-sharp mental faculties, he was a good worker, tireless really, so we let him stay and allowed our member the minor distraction of keeping an eye on him. However, she slackened in her nighttime-watch duties and fell asleep while on lookout. We weren't attacked that night, but one error could cost everyone here their lives, so she was punished and then asked to leave."

There's genuine-looking regret and sadness on his face as he relays this story, and Morgan feels herself beginning to doubt her initial impression. Discipline, after all, is one of her best companions, and she completely understands the logic of what he's described. One slip at the wrong time these days, and the shit hits the fan in a hurry. *Is it possible,* she thinks, *that Jack's crazier than I realized and maybe mistook something?* With some conscious effort, she lowers her guard just a bit.

"Will you join us for a meal? You're obviously on a journey of your own, but we can offer you food and drink and some fellowship for a while. You're welcome to stay the night here, too, if you choose. Stay a bit, please. I'd like to hear your story and tell you more of ours."

Morgan nods, figuring there's no harm in recharging her batteries and supplies since she gave Jack her remaining food and water, and this will save her a few moments of scavenging elsewhere. There's no way she's going to reach New York today, so she's going to need a couple of meals, at least. "Outside the walls though. No offense," she adds.

Marcus looks at her closely again, his interest in her very apparent this time, and a spot of anger or disappointment dances across his eyes. But then he shrugs and turns back to the crowd and begins dispensing orders to bring some tables, food, and water out. Everyone aside from the two bodyguards scramble quickly into motion, scurrying into the fortress and bringing out a series of picnic tables and food. The two guards watch her heavily for a few moments, but then they turn their attention away and to the perimeter, scanning the adjacent houses and street for danger. She's pleased to note that they do not step farther away from the walls than the car or between it and her. If she needs to leave in a hurry—because this isn't a safe place as Jack warned or they're attacked—she wants nothing in the way. The existence of walls and many armed people isn't a great sign for the ratio of people-to-monsters in the area, so she, too, keeps a sharp eye out.

Marcus seats himself first at the head of one of the tables and then gestures for her to take the seat to his right. Afterward, everyone else sits and tucks into the food, except for a pair of women in their twenties, one of whom is very pretty in a delicate way. She has pale, fair skin, completely unblemished save for the lingering shadow of a bruise around her left cheekbone, though that's mostly obscured by the straight hair that nearly reaches her waistline and hides most of her oval-shaped face. The other young woman is short, heavyset, and blonde, and she scurries this way and that, making sure all are happy in a blur of chatter and movement—so she's a people pleaser. These two serve the others. Soup is a staple here, too, but it tastes fresh instead of canned. When she remarks on that, Marcus tells her they farm some of the land within the walls as well as gather from the massive farms outside the suburbs for fresh vegetables and meat if they come across a cow. It's delicious, and she eats more than she plans, filling her stomach with the rich broth and al dente carrots, peas, and corn. Marcus eats little, instead choosing to fill her in on the story of the group.

He'd been living in one of the houses that's now enclosed by the walls when it all happened. A general contractor by trade, he secured the entire ground floor of his house with plywood and rebar once the first waves of zombies had brought their modern-day blitzkrieg to Middle America (and everywhere else). After ensuring he always had somewhere safe to go, he went searching for other survivors and supplies and brought both back to his house. Once he found too many people to fit in one house, he secured a second house in the same manner and then a third. Moving between houses exposed them to risk, and since there are huge construction supply places nearby and cinder blocks are simple and fast to build with, he decided to build the fort they now sit outside. He enlisted all the other able-bodied people and mapped out how many houses to enclose, and they built it all in about a week of very long days, alternating between building and guarding the builders. As she's seen, there are six houses on this side, and he tells her there are a total of sixteen in the enclosure. There aren't enough people to fill all those houses, but he explains that he wanted to overbuild and, therefore, have more than adequate room and be able to offer safety to anyone else who comes around over time.

"We do have fairly strict rules, of course, as well as significant consequences for violations of those like I said earlier," he explains. "But they were established for the good of the group. No one goes outside the walls in anything smaller than groups of five, everyone learns to use firearms, everyone takes their turn at watch, and all have a share of work to gather provisions. We all work together to survive together, and after some time, we've grown to what you see now, with me picked to remain as the leader once people saw what I'd done." There's some pride plus a dash of arrogance in his voice as he says this last part.

She can understand why people would follow someone who provides for and protects them, not to mention someone who looks and sounds like him. He's a natural leader. Despite her misgivings, she's found herself nodding in agreement with much of what he says without being conscious of it. History is littered with natural leaders though, some of them better than others. *Which category does he really fall into?* she wonders. *The ones who serve or the ones who expect subservience?*

Marcus asks her few questions, seemingly more absorbed in the explanation of their society's background. She offers the polite minimum in her replies, giving nothing about where she specifically came from or where she's going other than to "upstate New York to see if any family survived." Like most men, he's obviously very attracted to her, but she pays no particular attention to his roving eyes as they drift again and again over her contours since she's long become accustomed to inspection and admiration. After some time, she feels the need to use the bathroom and asks how they handle all that since the plumbing isn't going to work properly without power.

"Ah, that's one thing we haven't quite figured out yet. Power, that is. There are plenty of generators available, of course, but their noise makes the zombies nuts, and they prowl the walls endlessly, moaning and trying to get in, so we've discarded that as a solution. But for plumbing necessaries, in addition to the big construction supply site, we have a manufacturer of port-a-johns nearby. We've got a fresh set of those off in the southeastern corner of the compound, away from the occupied houses for privacy and, well, fragrance management."

He waves a hand casually off toward the fort, but it means going inside. Morgan doesn't like that. It won't take someone more than a few seconds to move the bus while she's indisposed, and then she'll be trapped.

She isn't happy about this, but then her stomach gurgles, twisting around like it's going to reject the food, so her decision is made. She isn't going to run off behind the nearest tree, so she hops up from the table and walks past the bus, through the walls, and quickly spots the line of blue water closets down one inside wall. There's no one inside the wall that she can see—the entire population is out at the picnic. Hurrying now, she enters the first one she comes to and does her business, relieved that it isn't an upset stomach but just a normal visit.

When she exits, she comes abruptly face-to-face with the pretty woman who has been serving lunch. Startled and already edgy, Morgan almost reaches around her back to withdraw the pistol, but the look of nervous fear on the woman's face tells her there's no threat here. She's obviously afraid, glancing over her shoulder and then spinning back to face Morgan. "He lies, you know," she says quickly and softly, constantly turning back toward the gap in the wall to ensure no one is coming. "All of it. No one voted him the leader—he just is. You need to leave. He likes you, which isn't good. I know. He used to like me too."

"What do you mean?" Morgan asks, her head spinning again, unsure which questions to ask first. "Used to like you?"

"Tribute. *Every* female pays tribute to him or his thugs for 'the privilege of safety,'" she says while making air quotes. "It's either submit or be forced, and then you're made to leave. That's the punishment for every infraction: you're stripped bare in front of everyone and kicked outside the walls with no supplies, no clothes, nothing. An example to others, plus whatever else his sick mind gets out of it."

"Tribute," Morgan says, neither liking the taste of the word in her mouth nor the idea of it in her mind, knowing what it means here, and is both disgusted and furious. Jack had been right.

"Yes. He's not a monster about it, not rough, and it's only once a month, but the other two ...." She shudders and then keeps talking. "One of them might actually be gay since he's never been able to do anything, or maybe he doesn't like the idea but is just going along with it. The other one though, the one who had the dog—he's horrible. Rough hands. He grabs and pinches until it hurts and seems to get off when we're in some pain. He's a fucking animal is what he is. Marcus lied about what happened with Jack, too, or most of it. Connie refused her turn at tribute with Marcus—she didn't fall asleep at the wall—and so he dragged her into the street, stripped her, and began to beat her in front of everyone until Jack stepped in and interfered. He went absolutely batshit at seeing Connie being degraded and hit, and because he knew she was going to be expelled, he tried to kill Marcus with his sword. Marcus swatted that aside, but he was so furious at the insubordination, he had Jack hauled outside the walls and chased away. Then Connie was pushed outside and chased away, too, from the other entrance. One of the houses in the back is the only other way out. The front door is locked but not barred like all the others, so we have an escape in case those things ever get inside the walls."

The woman licks her lips, turns back toward the space between the walls to check and see if they're being observed, and nervously pushes past Morgan toward one of the toilet stalls. "I can't say any more. They'll be suspicious already since we've both been gone for a few minutes. You need to go back first, and I'll wait a couple more so they don't think we were talking. I don't want to be punished and thrown out."

"But wait. You mean you'd rather stay here and pay this 'tribute' than escape and be free?" Morgan asks, utterly flabbergasted.

"It's safe here. We get attacked by them sometimes," she explains, waving an arm toward the outside world, "but the walls are tall. We shoot them pretty easily when they come, and we haul the bodies away the next day. None of us have been killed by a zombie for close to a year. The tribute was bad at first, it was, but you kind of get used to it. I just think of something else, and it's over pretty soon. They are men, after all. I'm safe and not dead. That's a decent deal nowadays," she rationalizes, but Morgan is speechless. This explanation runs contrary to everything she holds in her core being—"submission" isn't a word in her vocabulary.

The woman steps up onto the threshold of the nearest port-a-john and stands there for a moment, holding the door. "I have to go, and you do too. Whatever you do, don't accept his offer to spend the night. That's usually how he traps visitors who can't decide about staying. He decides for them. You were smart to leave your car outside the walls. Go back now, please. I don't want to get in trouble." She turns and closes the door, and Morgan stands there with her hands on her hips, fuming with anger at what she's just heard, at Marcus for abusing his power, and at this woman and the other inhabitants for being mindless followers.

At first, she considers waiting for the woman to come out, marching back to the group, and taking charge at gunpoint. She could let anyone out who chooses to leave, take one or two of them with her in the car, and set these people free. She could simply shoot Marcus and his goons, figuring if she surprises them, she'll be able to take down the two guards quickly and then handle Marcus and tell the rest to do what they want. But there's doubt in her mind. There aren't many people left, and killing any of them seems wanton. If she goes back there and starts shooting, the chances are good that a lot of people could be hurt or killed, and she isn't sure if only the two obvious bodyguards are on Marcus's side. It's one thing to wade into a pack of zombies, with their fairly slow movements and lack of strategic thought, but it would be another to fight at least three men, if not more.

An abrupt *thump* from the blue plastic startles her, followed by a muffled but urgent "Go, please" from inside, and impels her into motion. As she walks back, a sobering thought adds on top of her other hesitations: What if she tries to rescue these people and none of them leave with her? What if they're all accepting the submission to the rules, the paying of occasional tribute and confinement, in exchange for safety, security, and, like Marcus said, sanctuary? Like people trapped in their jobs, those working for someone else, not liking it but too fearful of change to even find out what lay outside. She's long held the opinion that most people are sheep just wanting someone to tell them what to do, how to do it, how to think, and so on. There aren't many who march to the beat of their own drum. This isn't something she can handle on her own, but as she closes in on the nearest table and decides that leaving sooner rather than later is a good move given she just received reinforcement of Jack's warning, she also makes a promise to herself that she intends to keep.

"Everything all right?" Marcus asks with a raised eyebrow. He has to know the women have at least passed one another, so he must be curious.

"Oh, yeah. I got a little turned around once I got behind the walls and wandered around for a couple of minutes, but that woman who was bringing food out at lunch found me and got me to the bathrooms. Just in time, too, luckily," she replies with a self-deprecating grin, wanting to downplay the time lapse and keep his guard down. She needs to accomplish two things: keep the other woman off his radar and get the heck out of Dodge.

Marcus looks at her silently for a moment or two, his eyes leaving hers to gaze at the space in the wall, clearly pondering whether he buys her story or not. She sees a small nod of his head, as if he's made some decision, and then the megawatt smile lights his face once more. "Why don't you stay with us? Or, at least, stay with us tonight? It's getting on in the day, and if you're going to New York, there is no way you'll make it before nightfall. I doubt that sleeping in that car will be comfortable … or safe." Morgan notices that besides speaking to her, he ensures his voice is loud enough for all to hear, reminding them that they're safe thanks to his benevolence. "We'd be *thrilled* to have you."

Wow, not even trying to be that subtle about it. Then again, men usually have the subtlety of a piano thrown off a skyscraper. Sometimes that's okay, but if anything, he confirms what the woman told her. This isn't a place of true safety, so it's time to go. *Now.* "Thank you, but no. I'm anxious to get back on the road and get closer to New York, and one night in the car won't be a problem. I appreciate the meal and the story. You've got a nice place here, good people. I wish you luck." She pauses as a thought strikes her, mischievous Morgan bubbling to the surface. "Anyone want to come with me? I have room for one more. Maybe someone else has family in New York, or …" another pause, "you just want a change of pace?"

That startles him, and there's no mistaking the anger on his face this time. She's put him in a shitty position. If he forbids anyone from going with her, it will be proof that he's a liar, but if he lets someone go, all his secrets will be exposed by that person, and he'll lose some control over them. She smiles (internally) and waits to see what happens next.

Standing up, Marcus speaks quickly to his flock, spreading his arms again, and effortlessly counters her. "Our guest, Morgan, has extended a generous offer while declining ours. If any of you would like to go with her in an impractical sports car to an unknown destination in New York, feel free to step forward. If more than one of you would like to leave,

I will choose which one gets to go." He turns and makes eye contact with each member of the group as he speaks, the challenge readily apparent, as is the threat. He is definitely a clever fellow.

For a moment, Morgan almost impulsively speaks up to defend herself and to say she's going to an *actual* safe place hidden on top of a hill to find her brother, but then she thinks it's smarter to listen and watch this time since she's just been outmaneuvered. Fighting hard to keep her face impassive, she stews in silence. She looks at the woman who told her so much. She had begun to step forward when Morgan made her offer, but as soon as Marcus added the twist, she froze. She's now at the rear of the crowd with fear in her eyes and staring at Morgan over the shoulders of the people in front of her. She shakes her head gently from side to side, a silent admonition for putting Marcus— all of them, for that matter—in an awkward spot. Morgan also scans the crowd and makes eye contact with the people assembled in front of her. Some of the crowd have a look of disdain in their eyes for the single woman driving around in a red sports car and trying to trick them, some of their eyes show nothing other than mild interest in however this turns out, and most of the younger females' eyes show fear—of staying or going, Morgan has no idea. Despite the stories all the eyes are telling, all the mouths keep silent. No one wants to take the risk of being the one not chosen if more than one person moves forward, so they all hold still. None of them are going to leave.

"Well," Marcus says, turning back to her, "looks like you came alone and are leaving alone. I'm glad you came to visit and see our place. You're welcome to come back if you don't find what you're looking for outside. I'll walk you to your car. Boys! Bring some water, food, and gasoline for Morgan to take with her. I wouldn't want it to be said we weren't generous, even if our hospitality isn't fully accepted."

They walk slowly back to the waiting car. Morgan opens the driver's door and stands for a moment, facing him. With his back to the crowd, his height and bulk shield her from viewing them and vice versa. She wants to say something, anything, to help her purge the anger she has inside. She's boiling mad at being outsmarted, at him for what he's created here, and at those in the group who turn the other way even though they know it's wrong.

But there are no words, not for her anyway. Leaning in close to her, he speaks *sotto voce*, "I could keep you here, you know."

Morgan holds eye contact with him, unblinking, and slowly reaches around to draw her pistol from its hiding place. Holding it close so his pals can't see it, she nudges the barrel of it firmly into his crotch, hard enough that he grunts quietly. "You could try," she whispers back, intimately. "Next time you have a visitor, maybe your clowns should search them for weapons. Security 101, you smug asshole."

He steps back, away from her, the flames of anger all over his face. She's evened the score a little bit and then thinks of one more thing. Her grandfather taught her at a young age to whistle "like a goddamn air-raid siren," according to her grandmother, and she does so now. The dog pops up from where he's been lying in the shade, trots over to her, and hops into the car to curl up in the passenger seat. "And I'm taking your little dog too." Always the last word.

Marcus just stares at her.

So Morgan leaves and returns to the road, a day and a half of driving remaining. She rolls the windows down as she makes her way back toward the highway, trying to let the tension of the last few hours fly out into the mostly abandoned city. Recalling the promise she made to herself earlier, she says it out loud, making it real.

"I'll be back."

Then she snickers, thankful she didn't say it in an Austrian accent.

CHAPTER 9

S unrise blazes to life in Pennsylvania on packing day, throwing long shadows across the yard. Amy is still sleeping in Eve's room while Ned and Eve bring their modest supplies out to the red pickup truck. Ned's mechanical skills have come in handy over the winter as he's run the truck periodically to keep the battery fresh, added fuel treatment to prevent water buildup, and checked all fluids again in the past few days.

Even though they have no more than one hundred miles to cover between here and New York, he says it's better to be prepared than rudely surprised. He's now checking the tires for pressure, even the spare, and Eve is thankful since these aren't things she would have considered. Her husband had been the car person—as in, he'd been the one to take the cars to the dealership if anything was wrong—and before him, her father had taken care of the cars she owned.

Once the truck's bed is fully packed with their food, water, and weapons, they go back indoors to collect anything else that may come in handy in the future. Eve moves without being quiet into her bedroom since she wants Amy to wake up soon so they can get on with their day. Peering at the photos on the bookshelves in the faint light, she scans them one more time and decides that, even though she's never going to come back, she's content to leave her past behind once and for all when they close the front door. There are only two things she decides to bring. One of them is her father's jacket, last worn during their conversation when she'd decided to stay here and watch him die instead of leaving with the rest of the group. It had fit both of the men well, and she thinks it will be something of a housewarming gift to carry along to New York. Plus, it smells like her father, like the Old Spice aftershave he'd worn since she was a young child. The other is a rather sinful yellow bikini that's cut high in the front and small in the back. It's the only one of the few that have lingered unworn for years in the dresser drawers that still fits her; she's tried all the suits on, knowing the weather will get warmer soon, and she certainly isn't going to skinny-dip in the lake. *DeeDee might have done so*, she thinks. *That would have undoubtedly been an impressive display.* She finds herself both excited and nervous to regroup with her friends. She tucks the suit inside one of the deep jacket pockets and then nudges Amy to life and opens the blinds to finish the job of waking her up. Amy groans and rolls over, eyes heavy with sleep, but then she clambers out of the bed readily enough since she's just as anxious to change locations and have a companion of her own age.

They all finally make their way out to the truck and pile into the cab, Ned driving, Amy in the middle. Just before

Ned starts it up, Eve tells them to wait for a second and steps back out to stand in the driveway. Her emotions about leaving this place for good—the time with her father, the decision he'd made, and the end of his life—all consume her for a moment, and she's nearly sick to her stomach with the wrench of sadness twisting in her body. Something tells her that of all the major stages she's been through in life—going to college, getting married, getting divorced, and then whatever this new reality can be called—this is the most significant. Everything's going to stay here, frozen in perpetuity, and she's going to begin the newest chapter of her life. There will be no more looking back like she's done too often in the past. She sends a silent prayer that it's all going to be okay.

Ned no sooner pulls out of the driveway and drives a few hundred feet down the street when they see it. A zombie, all by itself, shuffling up the road toward them and in little apparent hurry. Amy gasps and ducks down deeper into the blanket she dragged out of the house earlier.

"What the ...?" Ned says, keeping his eyes firmly on the intruder. "Just one ... that's not too common."

"Yes, you're right," Eve says, "but it's been a cold winter, so maybe some of them have died off and split up, I guess? Who can tell? They're not that predictable to begin with, so who can say what's normal?"

Ned taps his fingers on the steering wheel as she speaks and then gives an abrupt nod and climbs out of the truck. The zombie is still about a football field away from them, moving steadily but slowly.

"Ned! What are you doing?" Eve shouts across the cab and out the driver's window. "Get back in the truck, and let's just get out of here!"

"No, not yet," he replies without looking at her as he makes his way toward the back of the vehicle and pulls blankets and other items piled in the bed out of the way while his hands search for something. His eyes remain focused on the zombie the whole time. "I've got a confession to make: I've never killed one of them. All I did was hide and avoid them this entire time. I need to kill one just so I know I can do it, so I can pull my weight."

"That's stupid! You already pull your weight. You took care of the fire and the truck. Get back in here! I want to go, now."

"No. I don't do all the stuff *he* does, your friend in New York. You've told me the stories about the dozens of zombies you've seen him kill. I need to be able to do that too. For me, for you." He draws a rifle out, fumbles with the safety, sights carefully down the barrel, and fires at the zombie now inside of eighty yards.

And misses horribly.

He curses under his breath and fires again. Closer this time; Eve sees a bit of dirt flick up from the road about ten feet to the right of the zombie. The zombie, for its part, strides onward, maybe a little faster now.

"Shit," Ned murmurs with a less steady voice. He draws the gun up to his shoulder, rests the barrel on the side mirror of the truck, and fires again.

And misses again.

Mostly.

This shot nicks the zombie in the left shoulder, the impact flinging it back briefly but not slowing its progress. He actually seems to have picked it up yet another notch, now going into a jog.

Amy gives a little scream and reaches over to push at Eve's arm, shouting, "I wanna go right now! Pleasepleaseplease get me out of here, Eve!"

Eve hadn't been aware of it, but after the second shot, she'd stepped out of the truck, too, and she now realizes she's standing in the street with the door ajar in front of her. "Ned, come on! This isn't proving anything except that you're a terrible shot! Amy is terrified, I'm frightened, too, and we should just get back in the truck right now and get the hell out of here."

He doesn't respond; he's still hunched over the gun and sighting for another shot. She needs to run behind the truck in order to reach him without accidentally being shot at, so she turns toward the rear of the truck ...

And freezes.

"Oh no."

Despair makes the words fade into the breeze.

Over a dozen zombies—big, small, newer, older, and with necrotic skin peeling from their faces—are only a couple of car lengths behind them. They've been creeping silently toward them while they've been distracted by the single zombie. Eve hadn't heard a bit of sound as they approached.

She shrieks at the top of her lungs, and that finally gets Ned's attention. He spins to see what has scared her.

"Ohmygod, get in!" He tosses the rifle into the bed and practically dives into the truck, slamming the door behind him and fidgeting with his seat belt of all things. Eve jumps in, too, and twists around to watch the horde behind them through the back glass.

Muuuuuuuhhhhh!

The mob breaks into a run, closing in on the back bumper in just a few steps.

"Ned, get us the fuck out of here!" Eve says, again at the top of her lungs even though she's right next to him, trying to prod him to move faster. He is still wrestling with the seat belt, which strikes her as total insanity in this moment.

Amy is tucked down as low as she can be in the seat, head covered by the blanket that muffles her sobs. The first *thump* against the truck doesn't come from behind them but rather in front as the Trojan Horse launches itself onto the leading edge of the hood just as Ned shifts into drive. The truck lurches forward, spraying loose gravel on the crowd now chasing them down the street. The zombie up front scrabbles desperately for purchase on the smooth surface, and Eve sees a fingernail peel off as it tries to get a grip on the seam between the fender and hood.

Ned does his part now that he has the vehicle moving and slews the steering wheel from side to side in an effort to dislodge their unwelcome passenger. At first, it hangs on tenaciously, a few fingers stubbornly clinging to the base of the antenna, but as they gather speed, it slowly slides away from their line of sight, fingers clasping open air before it falls beneath the front of the truck. They don't run it over with

the tires, but the heavy *thunk-thump* as it passes underneath is convincing. Eve spins around again in her seat to see it tumble over a few times on the asphalt and finally come to rest like a soggy rag doll. "Gone ... he's gone, and we're okay," she says. "Amy, we're okay, honey. You can come out."

The shivering child emerges from underneath the blanket and collapses into Eve's arms, shaking as she cries on Eve's shoulder. Eve is shocked at how strong her grappling arms are as she seeks comfort.

Ned looks over, the fear in his eyes still there. "Jesus ...." is all he says.

None of them notice the faint smell of gasoline.

***

Two hours later, just after passing the welcome sign for the town they're heading to, the truck starts to stutter, and the engine abruptly quits.

Ned mutters a "now what?" and lets the truck coast to the shoulder of the road out of habit and looks down at the dials of the dashboard. "The gas gauge is empty, but that makes no sense. It was full when we left. I checked that when I was getting ready. I don't get it." He steps out, leans down—Eve watches with a moment of panic as she recalls their episode with the zombie that clung to the bottom of the *other* truck when they'd been leaving North Carolina—and curses before leaning back into the cab. "The gas line has a small leak in it. I can see it dripping still. That thing must have nicked it somehow when we ran it over. Well shit. Now what do we do?"

Eve thinks back for a moment on the directions and description of the town. It isn't very large, and the road leading to the cabins is off this route, so it can't be more than a couple of miles from here to there. The day is sunny and cool, with sparse clouds littering the otherwise clear sky, and there are no zombies in sight, so she figures they should be able to walk there in less than an hour. What's one more hour in a journey that feels like it has started ages ago in that suburban neighborhood in North Carolina?

Making up her mind, she says, "Let's just grab what we truly need, like some snacks, water, and weapons, and hike it. It can't be far now. The directions say it's maybe a mile after you cross the town line before the turn off and then another mile to reach the cabins." She hops out and busies herself with unloading a few things from the back, filling a backpack—now *de rigueur* as an accessory—with supplies and tucking a pistol into an outer pocket. Amy jumps down as well and fills her own One Direction backpack with a few things, though no weapon for her yet. Ned stands for a moment with an annoyed expression on his face at the inconvenience of having to hit the bricks and then gathers his own items. They start off walking up a gentle rise that stretches out for at least half a mile ahead of them, feeling the sun warm the asphalt and their backs as they go. It's actually a good day for a walk. Eve leads the way, settling them into a good pace and drifting off into her thoughts.

She holds some doubt now that they're here—or almost here—about whether everyone else is still alive. It was a nasty winter, especially without power, and the zombies are always to be reckoned with since they horribly outnumber the survivors. And she admits to herself she's nervous about arriving and finding that things have changed as Ned suggested. The largely unspoken pattern she and DeeDee had followed before they left North Carolina, of alternating sleepover nights, was something she's missed these last few months even though she had Amy in her bed most of the nights. She had enjoyed being tucked up against him and feeling the comfort of his warm, hard-muscled body against hers, knowing that he was going to protect all of them with everything he had to give. She knows DeeDee had been attracted to him as well, and she suspects he had been attracted to both of them, making the whole thing very complicated. He looked at both of them with a measure of admiration and embarrassment obvious on his face. It had to have been difficult for him to have two attractive ladies come to his bed and to maintain the respect he clearly had for women. The cold months and one-on-one time may well have tipped the scales between him and DeeDee. She knows DeeDee won't remain circumspect about her feelings for long, but there's nothing she can do about it. Right now, the main goal is to rejoin the group and find sanctuary.

The sound of a car startles her out of her reverie as she reaches the top of the rise. A car! Once so common, now an anachronism in a mostly silent world. It's loud, the engine waxing and waning in volume as the driver changes speeds in the distance. All three of them turn to look at the road behind them beyond the distant truck. The gleam of sunlight off the windshield is the first thing that comes into view, and then the red car comes closer.

"Corvette, new one," Ned says.

The pitch of the exhaust dwindles for a split second—the driver must have seen their forms silhouetted at the top of the hill—and then rises sharply as they clearly hit the gas again. The gap closes rapidly, and Eve guesses the car is traveling at well over 80 miles an hour. The three of them shuffle off to the shoulder as it approaches, and Ned waves his hands above his head, signaling the driver to stop.

The driver, a woman wearing large sunglasses with a mass of dark hair flowing in a whirling shroud in the windy cockpit, never slows a bit or turns her head to look at them. The only acknowledgment of their existence is a brief blast of the car's horn. As the car passes by, thunderous exhaust howling, Eve glimpses a dog in the passenger seat: a big German shepherd happily dangling its head out of the top of the car, tongue out and waving blissfully in the wind. A moment later, the red bullet is gone around a bend, spent gas lurking in the air behind it, the noise of its passage fading as rapidly as it arrived. Eve, Ned, and Amy look at one another, perplexed at the sight of the car to begin with and then the driver's indifference to three survivors on the side of the road.

Eve fumes. *That bitch actually honked the horn at us! Didn't stop to see if we needed help. No, why do that for your fellow man, especially when there aren't many of them left? She just honked the damn horn!*

Amy speaks up, changing the subject and getting them back to the task at hand. "This has been the weirdest day ever. Let's go. I'm tired of walking already, and I'm hungry. I think I have to pee, too, and I'm not doing it on the side of the road."

So they resume their walk, following the route the Corvette took. Eve's anger eventually starts to dissipate. People being rotten to one another isn't a new thing, after all. She just hopes the cabin isn't far.

CHAPTER 10

Only a few days have passed since first Top, then Amelie, and then DeeDee have been removed from my life (and theirs). I haven't spent the time doing much other than moping around the family property that now feels even bigger than when I was a child. I've always been comfortable being something of a loner in the past even though I've never actually been alone—people could've been found everywhere I went—but now I just rattle around the place. Sure, I have my dog Ajax for company, but he isn't much of a conversationalist, though he is, admittedly, a superb listener.

***

After DeeDee died, I briefly considered suicide because all of my people were dead, and I was miserable. But I decided to stay here, in *my* place and continue to fight. Once I was sure the zombie pack in the nearby town hadn't followed me back to the cabin, I buried her in the family plot down the hill. DeeDee may not have been blood, but she was like family to me, so she deserved a full measure of respect. It was a bit of a drive to get down to the ancient cemetery in the middle of town, and I struggled with whether to put her in the front of the truck or in the bed. As was his wont, the dog was riding in the bed; I hesitated to put her back there because that felt disrespectful, as if she were so much cargo. The idea of having a corpse sitting next to me up front, however, was deeply unsettling. Too much of an imagination—combined with plenty of horror movies over the years, not to mention the one I have been living for some time now—put the thought in my head that at some point during the drive, she would move or say something. I tried covering her with a sheet, but that actually made it worse, so I kept watching her out of the corner of my eye for motion. After only a minute of driving, I finally stopped the truck, picked her up, and lay her down in the back seat.

Watch out for fingers creeping over the back of the seat! Is that a rustling sound I hear? It seems lots of the bodies these days do get back up after all. Oh ho, you are far too easy to mess with, my friend. Sometimes, it's barely fun. Yup, I'm still here, your one and only. Onnnneeee is the loneliest number. C'mon, everybody, sing!

Digging a grave by hand had been a miserable task. There were more rocks than dirt in that part of the country, and the ground was hard from the still retreating winter. Because of that, it took forever and prolonged the emotional drain. I was inside my head with that goddamn gleeful doomsday voice for way too long, and it happily mocked me about what my future was going to be. Despite the wondrous idyll of my location, the fact remained that I was going to be in the middle of fucking nowhere all by myself. Indeed, it was a relaxing and peaceful and largely safe place so far, though there was the remnant of the pack to be dealt with harshly—I was going to enjoy plotting how to remove all of them as noisily as I could—but I feared that peace and quiet wouldn't be much stimulation after a few months, and I'd go nuts atop that small mountain, especially if I made it to another winter. The prospect of being trapped in the cabin again but alone this time was chilling.

Really? "Winter" and "chilling"? That's what you're going to go with? Gee, why don't you go ahead and quit your day job and become a writer since you're so very clever? Just go find the nearest funny (or not funny) farm now and save the bother of waiting around for crazy to completely show up.

After some hours, I eventually finished a shallow grave. I carefully lifted DeeDee from the back of the truck and lowered her into the opening. I'd already said goodbye earlier, and words failed me now, so I just stood there for a moment of silence and then slowly and carefully covered her with the displaced soil. One thing I could not bring myself to do was pat the dirt down—again, it felt somehow lacking in respect—so I left the mound above her body.

With that task done, I thought about what I needed to do next. Kill the zombies and find some company—got it. But in what order? Go try to find Eve, bring her back, kill the zombies, and then play "little house on the lake" thereafter? Or kill the zombies to make it the safe little house on the lake first, then find Eve?

If she was still alive.

It had been a monstrous winter, and she'd been by herself with her dying father in a town with some zombie presence. Who knew if she survived? Regardless, I had to go find out if she was in trouble, and then the zombies would be in trouble. I swore to the assorted moss-covered gravestones of the dead, silent sentries that I was going to avenge DeeDee and all those who had also succumbed to the creeping death that plagued the world. No small promise.

As I drove away from the town, I remembered that Top's and Amelie's bodies were still in the meadow, Mabel's, too, if the zombies had left them undisturbed. They hadn't been carrion eaters so far. Fresh kills, yes—those were eaten down to the bone like Top, but anything that had been lying around for a bit, they left alone. I was exhausted from burying DeeDee, but the sense of responsibility overwhelmed my fatigue, and I turned the truck toward town and steeled myself for burying the three of them that same day.

Nothing had bothered me while I was doing so, and the meadow, too, now holds three mounds spread out across it, interrupting the green swaths of long grass. Ajax stood guard, scanning the tree line patiently while I worked to inter my friends and say farewell. I hoped they were somewhere better as I finished, surveying the peaceful space that had turned into a battlefield and then, like all battlefields, had turned into a cemetery. The soil had been more cooperative there for the grisly work, but it was still deep dusk by the time I dragged myself into the truck and then back home. Without bothering to undress, I fell into bed and slept like a teenager, dreamlessly for once.

I rose from bed far later than usual the next morning, though I didn't notice until I made my way unsteadily outdoors, as if oppressed by a well-deserved hangover, and saw the height of the sun. Bright in the clear sky, it shone down between the hemlock branches to dot the open space between the cabin and garage with fingers of light. I was terribly foggy in the head and sore of body and soul. There had been four of us, plus the dogs, living safely and happily here, and then that happiness was ripped from me, or all of us, almost too suddenly to absorb. I stood at the foot of the porch steps and stared mindlessly out across the lake I'd looked over my entire life, trying to find comfort in the view and the memories of all that had happened before the most recent events. It was hard to conjure up an optimistic view of the future. All those fond memories included other people, such as family members and Morgan in particular.

***

On top of the prior day's sweaty work, it has been a day or two since my last bath. I strip where I am, shedding my gravedigger's clothes in a trail behind me, and walk to the shore of the lake with Ajax trailing at my heel. It's going to be cold, I know that, but it isn't as if anyone will notice the shrinkage. The water by the retaining wall at the shore is shallow, no more than a foot deep, so I can't go for the full, all-at-once plunge and have to wade in to midthigh, which really sucks, before I can dive forward into the bracingly cold depths.

As I come to the surface, shivering already, I hear a sound. A car sound, and an American-performance car sound at that. High-end performance cars from European or Asian manufacturers—aside from the wild Italian exotics—sound languorous in their exhaust note, like they're afraid to disturb the peace. American cars go right the hell ahead and disturb the peace, no apologies asked or needed. The deep rumbling of a V8 engine rising only gradually and resting back to idle or barely above means the car is in the long driveway. Ajax is fully alert now, looking over toward where the driveway leads down to the lower level and the cabins, his hackles up in a bristling forest along his spine. He holds his ground and waits for me to scramble ashore and struggle to pull my jeans on over my wet skin.

Who could have found me? I haven't run a fire in a few days, so there's no telltale column of smoke to guide another survivor. This isn't exactly a scenic overlook marked down on the main road, and the One Way sign at the foot of the driveway tends to confuse people—when there had been people—and steer idle wanderers away.

On the bright side, a car means a person. For a moment, I think it may be Eve, but the sound is different than that of a truck; it's heavier somehow. Whatever—or whoever—it is, they're close since I can see the flash of sunlight off the windshield as they approach on the upper level. I can see now that it's a newest model Corvette, which pauses and then descends the driveway's last fifty feet, coasting to a rumbling stop in front of the garage. Due to the angle of the sun, I'm not able to see through the windshield, but the spatter of dead bugs and dust all over the nose tells of a long journey. I stand there shivering in just my jeans, without my typically handy .45, next to the mostly empty lean-to that stores firewood, so I slip my hand over the smooth handle of the axe resting inside one vertical post without being visible to the driver. Ajax continues to stand at alert, ready to explode at the intruder if prompted, and I feel better.

The car continues to idle for a moment or two, quivering gently with its raw power, and then is silenced. I see shadowy movement behind the steering wheel, and then the door finally opens. A statuesque woman with a riot of messy hair emerges, sweeps that hair up to the crown of her head with a pair of sunglasses, turns back to the interior of the car, and lets a huge German shepherd out of the passenger seat.

Morgan.

Out of all the people in the world. Showing up in a red Corvette. All the way from Colorado or wherever she moved to since the last time I'd spoken to her.

"Well, are you going to just stand there like an idiot with your mouth hanging open, or are you going to come greet your sister?" she asks as casually as if we just saw each other a week ago and the world forgot to come to an end. She's smiling a broad smile that lights her features with happiness but can't hide the passage of this most recent time, at least not from my eyes.

I step forward, and we're about to hug when Ajax surges between us to check out the other dog, bumping me almost off my feet as he nudges against my knee in passing. The two of them circle, doing the requisite sniff-the-parts routine, muscles tense and ready for a brawl, if needed. "Hey, boy, it's okay. They're friends," I say in a soothing voice, which is ignored while the dogs finish their getting acquainted shenanigans—Butt? Check. Nuts? Check. Okay, we're good to go—and then the new dog abruptly walks over and takes a leak against the outhouse, followed by Ajax doing the same. The two of them then trot off to explore, apparently satisfied with each other. "Nice car," I say as I close in on Morgan.

"Why does everyone say that?"

I fold my sister into my arms, feeling the hard muscles flexing beneath her clothes and smelling the familiar smell of her skin and hair that takes me back to our earlier years and brings a soft ache to my chest. I've been okay emotionally for the most part because I was alone in the beginning, then with strangers who quickly became close friends, but I had not been with family at all during this time. Aside from how I feel about my immediate family, I'm not a terribly emotional person, staying somewhat detached from them in favor of logic. Now, however, the weight of the fact that *everyone* I know is dead—save for my sister by some miracle—hits me hard, and I can't help the tears that pour out of my eyes. As I step back from her and hold her by the shoulders, I see she is also overcome with emotion. The two of us just stand there in the driveway, smiling at one another and crying at the same time, until finally getting our shit together and walking toward the main cabin.

In a gesture I can't explain as anything other than sibling intimacy, Morgan takes my hand as we walk the few steps, as if seeking solace in continued contact. My sister is here. My enigmatic, wild, maddening, temperamental, and ever-fascinating big sister is here, alive and with me. With a dog and a sweet Corvette.

"What's your dog's name?" she asks.

"Ajax."

"Nice. That's a badass name for a dog. Mine doesn't have a name that I know of, but I think I'm going to call him Jack. I met a guy on the way, a friend you could say, and his name was Jack. Jack the Pirate."

"Jack the Pirate? Not, like, *that* Jack the Pirate?" I ask, wondering where she came from. Last I'd known, she was in Colorado, but if I've learned anything over the years, nothing is impossible with my sister. A trip through Hollywood and running into a certain celebrity? I wouldn't put it past Morgan to run in circles like that; she's stunning and compelling, probably enough for the west coast famous crowd, though she thinks as highly of them as I do (not very). I think back to the most recent Jack I had the displeasure of meeting, feel a—tiny and quickly passing—twinge of guilt for what had happened, and then move on. He'd been a piece of shit, and I made too many mistakes with him, the biggest being trusting him.

Stifling a laugh, Morgan replies, "Well, he thinks he's a pirate for sure, but no, not the real one. Yeah, Jack works. Is it just you here?"

"Yes, I'm alone, but I wasn't up until a little while ago. Sit down. I'll get us some water and something to eat. We've got a lot to talk about." We're going to have all the time in the world, but I really want to fill her in.

She stops me as I'm about to go inside. "Wait ... Mom and Dad?"

"No. I was never able to get through to them after ... after it all started. I'd hoped they were going to be here when I arrived last year, but no. No sign that anyone from the family was here."

"Oh. Okay," she answers quietly.

I look at her as she stares out over the placid water of the lake, and I think I catch the barest shimmer in the corner of her eye before I duck indoors. I'm glad to see that. She's been at odds with our parents for most of her life, constantly going in the direction she was told or asked or begged *not* to go, always doing her own thing without regard for anyone, and I'd always been caught in the middle. I guess I've always assumed she loves our folks, but this quiet proof is good to see.

I throw a shirt on, go into the kitchen, and grab a glass of the spring water the two of us used to drink when we were children, which has its own distinct, instantly recognizable smell and taste, at least to me.

After bringing it outside and handing it to Morgan, she drinks deeply, finishing the glass in a single, long swallow and sets it down with a smile. "That's such good water. I thought I'd forgotten what it tasted like, but it just makes sense to my taste buds. Some things never change. It's just like when we were kids, isn't it?"

Nodding with a smile of my own, I say, "That's one part of why we came here. I knew it'd be mostly safe since there weren't many people up here to begin with, plus the cold winters, familiar ground, and all that. And, I figured if there was anywhere Mom and Dad would be, it would be here."

I pause for a minute, a little overcome now that Morgan is here. It's one thing when the draw of memories is just that. Memories. It's another thing to have someone who's such a huge part of those memories here with me, and it's a bittersweet feeling. There are no do-overs, especially not now, but like DeeDee used to be focused on, second chances are a great goal. I was so happy to have another chance to be with my sister.

"You just said 'we.' Who's 'we'?"

"That's a *long* story. Where do you want me to start?"

"I guess at the beginning, or the beginning of all … all this," she answers with a wave of her hand.

And so I tell her everything. All the way back to North Carolina, the golf course, the women being delivered by the Queen and her minions, the first Jack, the trip to Pennsylvania and leaving Eve, and finally about the more recent, and more painful, past with Top, Amelie, and DeeDee. I leave nothing out since there's never any filter between us nor any judgment. We've always simply been there for one another, for whatever reason, and none of the world's changes will influence that relationship. All relationships should be that simple and open. I talk for what feels like an hour and then reach the end.

She's quiet for a long moment when I finish and grab my own glass of water. I don't think I've done so much talking in over a year, but there was a lot to tell. Finally, she says, "Jesus. You've been through a lot. I'm sorry for your losses. That sounds a little hollow, but I don't know what else to say. All of your friends sounded like good people. I would have liked to have met them, all of them."

I wish she could have too. Maybe things would have turned out differently if she'd been here before the fateful days where Top and Amelie ran into the horde; Top and Mabel died while saving Amelie, only for Amelie to try and avenge them that following day and dying herself. They *were* good people, and my heart aches that their stories are over.

It's Morgan's turn to fill me in, and she takes me through her introduction to the zombies, the following year of hunting, and then her trip here, with a long explanation of meeting Jack the Pirate—I mean, really?—and going to the place in Kansas City and what's happening there. I can see she's still angry at this Marcus guy and the stomach-turning enclave he's created for his own benefit, but the very practical part of me acknowledges that he's also created safety for those people. I'm not sure I'm okay with practical me on that point, and I share her anger at what he's inflicting on the women. After everything, *everything* humans have been through—millions of people being savaged by insane mockeries of humans and eaten by them—here are people still taking advantage of women. I'm seething with outrage by the time she begins to explain her departure. It reminds me of the bullshit with Jack and the three assholes here last year, and the realization that I'm still burning with deep anger at those moments makes me fume. Women owe men *nothing*, not before and especially not now when we're all a fragmented minority on the planet.

Just as I'm starting to utter the words "road trip," the dogs race by the porch toward the driveway, low rumbles coming from their throats as they fly past in a furry blur of black and brown.

Now what?

I grab my trusty .45 from the small of my back where it seems to live at all times—I almost lost it once during a seated visit in the outhouse because I'd forgotten about it as I dropped my drawers, and I barely caught it before it tumbled into the refuse—sweep up the shotgun from where it always rests in the corner, and subconsciously check to make sure I have the KNIFE on my leg and spare magazines for the pistol rattling loose in my pocket. Morgan has no weapons with her on the porch aside from a machete in a holster-looking rig on her thigh, so I toss her a rifle from our grandfather's collection of guns. I keep a half dozen loaded weapons on the porch, just in case; if there's going to be a fight, I'm going to be ready. The crossbow DeeDee favored is on the porch, too, but it lacks the serious killing power of the guns, so there it sits while we trot off the edge of the porch and jog after the dogs to the foot of the driveway.

For the second time that day, I'm struck speechless. Standing at the base of the hill leading to the parking area of the driveway, held at bay by the two mammoth dogs snarling a warning, are two women—well, one woman and a kid who looks something like a Muppet exploding out of a hoodie—and one man. All three are carrying backpacks and are sweaty and slightly dirty, as if they've been hiking for a good while. The man is shakily pointing a revolver at one dog, then rotates to the other dog. As we come into sight, he swings it toward Morgan and me. The barrel wiggles like it's held by a man with palsy, and I'm more worried that he'll shoot someone by accident than on purpose. We drift to a stop at the sight of the gun and its unsteady holder. Stepping to his side, murmuring something in his ear, and gently grasping his forearm to lower the weapon is none other than Eve.

Eve.

Still alive.

Eve.

CHAPTER 11

Once she turns away from the man, Eve faces us and surprises me by marching right up to Morgan, who practically towers over her and is a bundle of muscles compared to Eve's build.

Eve, however, doesn't seem to give a shit about the mismatch and stops in front of Morgan.

"Nice *car*," she says angrily. "Thanks for the ride."

I shoot a questioning look at Morgan, who shrugs indifferently, not the least bit intimidated. "Sorry," she says, not sounding sorry at all. "How was I supposed to know you were coming here or that you were friends? Plus, where was I supposed to put the three of you, anyway? Two-seater, dog, driver, no room at the inn," she replies brusquely, looking down at Eve with a look I know well from our youth. The one that usually means Morgan's about to kick someone's ass.

Well, this is off to a great start. The two women stand there staring at one another, and I'm worried Morgan just might belt her—Morgan being Morgan, after all, and prone to, let's say, spontaneous displays of irrational and unpleasant behavior. I'm overwhelmed to see Eve, that she's safe, and I can barely contain the desire to hold her and confirm she's really here in one piece after the miserable winter and all the concerns I've had about her.

Need me to pinch you, sunshine? Yup, she's here, but notice there's a new dude in her life who may or may not have kept her warm all winter, so there's that. And, lest we forget, you happened to snuggle in tight with DeeDee a few times there in the chilly weather. I know. I saw. Looked like you were having fun. Good luck figuring all that shit out.

I shake off the jackass voice and then break in to the standoff and simply hug her, feeling her familiar shape in my arms, and a huge ball of worry slides off my shoulders. She wraps her arms around me and clutches me fiercely. I wait, enjoying the moment, but I can't help asking all the questions bubbling to mind. "I'm so glad to see you. I worried about you all winter. What happened with your father? Who are these two? You didn't walk the whole way here, did you? I thought the truck was running fine when we left?"

"This is Amy and Ned," she answers with a gesture to the other two, who are standing by about as awkwardly as can be, still bracketed by the dogs.

"Hey, Ajax, it's okay! These are friends. Relax." He looks at me, pads forward, nudges Ned in the crotch, then pushes his muzzle into one of the girl's hands for a pat. Satisfied with his version of hello, he trots up the driveway with Jack in tow.

"My father ... he died, like we knew he would, but he lived far longer than I thought, right up until the big snowfall. And then these two showed up at my door shortly after, and we spent the winter together, which was a good thing. I don't think I'd have made it alone. Who's that?" she asks with a nod toward Morgan, who's just watching. "And where is everybody else?"

I can't answer at first, not really wanting to. The way I lost everyone rubs on my emotions like sandpaper on a rug burn. Having just explained it all to Morgan, I'm wrung out already and still overwhelmed by Eve's arrival. So instead of saying anything, I just shake my head slowly.

"*No*," Eve whimpers in a low voice that drifts off into the breeze. "What happened? They're not … dead, are they?"

This time, I nod my head, holding her gaze and watching her eyes begin to tear up. I bring her back into my arms and feel long shuddering breaths rake through her chest. It's a long moment before she speaks again. "You'll have to tell me. I'm so … *so* sorry. For all of us. So much loss. It's not fair."

She sure has that right. We've already been through so much as a small group, from the alpha to the first Jack to the travels. But she's back with me, and there are five of us now plus two dogs. I'm not alone anymore. All in all, it's been a pretty damn good day. Wanting to make everyone comfortable, I gesture for them to make their way over to the porch. I look at Morgan over the top of Eve's head while we're walking and see she's still steamed, and perhaps a little jealous, but I shake that off, knowing she'll get over it.

Ned has been quiet throughout the greeting, but as we walk past the open door of the garage, he nearly shouts, "Is that what I think it is?"

I give him a puzzled look. "What do you mean?"

"It is … that's a 2800! And a CS! I haven't even seen one of those in at least a decade and certainly not in that condition. That's about the holy grail of BMWs for guys like me. Does it run?"

He sounds like an excited teenager, and I immediately warm to his enthusiasm. "No, I tried to start it, but it wouldn't turn over. Far as I know, it hasn't been running for at least five years, maybe more. I don't know enough about cars to get it going. Do you?"

"Heck yeah! I was a shade tree mechanic before … before, you know. BMWs were my specialty, but I mostly worked on recent 3 Series ones, nothing vintage or special like this. This is my absolute favorite! Can I work on it?"

"Sure! If you could get it going, it would mean a lot. It was our grandfather's car. Keys are in it, tools are in the garage too, but I don't think there's much in the way of mechanic's tools. More woodworking ones."

He almost jumps up and down, which is both fun and funny to see. Here's a guy who looks like an accountant with thinning hair and is wandering into his forties, and he's as fired up about the car as a sixteen-year-old getting his first set of wheels. He ducks into the garage and circles the car, head bobbing up and down as he inspects it. The rest of us walk up to the porch, and Eve and Amy drop their backpacks and settle into some of the wooden rocking chairs.

"Can we have something to eat and drink?" Eve asks. "We've had nothing for a few hours, and we had to walk a good way." Another accusatory glance toward Morgan, who ignores it.

"Of course." I go inside and crack open a couple of soup cans and set them to cooking on the grill, and then I busy myself getting a few more glasses for water. I bring those out and hand them around.

After knocking back her glass, Eve smiles and looks up at me. "Do you have anything stronger?"

I know the answer this time, unlike when we first met, and smile back at the memory. "Absolutely. Whiskey still good?"

A happy nod from her. Quizzical looks from Morgan and Amy.

Everything's going to be okay.

***

We spend the rest of the afternoon catching up, and each of us shares parts of our story the others don't know. Ned eventually pokes his head out of the garage after an hour or so and sits with us, though he frequently glances back at the car that isn't going anywhere, looking at it as if it were a mirage.

I don't go into *all* the details of the time since Eve and I last saw one another. I have to think some more about the right way to explain everything, and I also think it's a conversation for only the two of us. I don't feel any guilt over being with DeeDee, quite the opposite, nor do I feel like Eve and I should hurry to belong together in that same way. However, given the odd circumstances where they'd alternated sleeping (only) with me in the past, I feel Eve deserves the full story at the right moment in case she decides to do so again and there is more to it than sleeping.

***

That evening brings a dazzling sunset that leaks over the edges of the western tree line in a blaze of glorious colors painted on the bottom of the lingering clouds. It's something of a surprise to see such a vivid display because many of the sunsets since the end of (well, most of) mankind have been less colorful, and I suspect that much of the difference is due to the lower level of debris in the air. As the sunlight fades, the dark falls as sharply as it always does here, and I walk around the porch to light the kerosene lanterns that hang every few feet, breathing in yet another scent from childhood that reminds me of my father's Zippo lighter.

Avoiding the whiskey myself, I run a quick patrol up the driveway and around the lake with the two dogs to ensure we don't have any visitors. I'm thrilled we have a second dog and another physically capable person; it means that, with this new group, we won't have to always all stay together. Morgan or I can take a dog and check around while the other remains at the cabins on guard. Based on what I've seen of Ned's handling of the pistol, he isn't going to be a ton of help in a fight, but hopefully he can shepherd Eve and Amy to safety if needed. Eve hadn't been comfortable with weapons before we split up and, to my recollection, hadn't killed any zombies either, so she and the kid are out too. I'll have to think about some escape routes for them, where they can get to safety if we have invaders.

Time for that later. Right now, the sleeping arrangements need to be figured out.

I'm in the main cabin, and Ajax never moves from my room. Morgan waffles at first between the second cabin—where we always slept as kids—and the third—where we never slept since it only had a queen bed—because Eve explains that Amy sleeps with her, and Ned doesn't want to sleep in the main cabin with me or by himself in the third.

You're making my head hurt.

Final answer: Eve and Amy in the larger room with the queen bed in cabin two, Ned in one of the single beds in the other bedroom in the same cabin, and Morgan and Jack in the family room of the main cabin with me. I had offered her the bedroom, but she declined immediately, saying it creeps her out to sleep in the same bed our grandparents had. I'm not wild about all our real firepower being consolidated in one space, but it's a matter of a couple dozen steps to cabin two, so I figure I can get there in time. Plus, the two dogs will be our alarm.

Nothing happens that first night except for deep, restful sleep.

***

Nothing happens the next day either ... or the next day ... or the next. It's quiet as we all get settled in and find routines people always seem to prefer, consciously or otherwise. The weather is superb—clear and sunny and dry as it generally tends to be. I can rarely recall there being any rainy days when we visited as kids, which had probably been a blessing for our grandparents since we high-energy children weren't cooped up in too-small quarters. The whole place is built for being outdoors, and that's what we survivors do, with the exception of Ned, who's enthralled with the BMW and trying to get it running. He comes out for meals and some household chores and the periodic break, but otherwise, he is steadily banging and clanging away in the garage during daylight hours.

I've gone in a few times to chat with him and see his progress. I also wanted to get a feel for the man who's survived, rescued a young girl, and arguably helped Eve survive the death of her father and the winter's clutches but looks as capable in a mortal fight as a BB gun. He acknowledges me, talks lightly about whatever part he's working on, but he stays focused on the car and resurrecting it from inertia. Parts of the engine are scattered in apparent chaos, to my eyes at least, across the ancient workbench, covering the gouges and scars in the surface from generations of my family's projects. Overall, he seems nice enough, fairly unremarkable, but I feel I owe him a debt of thanks for helping Eve find her way here and give him a mental thumbs-up.

Morgan isn't as sure about him.

Every evening, as everyone settles for bed, Morgan and I stay up and talk just like when we were kids—though now, we don't have to whisper so our parents won't hear. We list the projects we need to complete, discuss the routes we should patrol the next day—we have the zombie group in town that's going to need to be eliminated if we can come up with a well-planned and safe way to do so—and catch up on the years that have passed since we were in the same place.

She isn't wild about Ned, deeming him to have an obsessive streak and disliking his detachment from the group, which is odd coming from a loner like Morgan. His disinterest in Amy also worries her, but she has trouble being specific as to why. "Just a feeling," she tells me.

Eve, however, she's come to like rather a lot. "Did you see the way she switched between soothing him down with the gun but then stomped right up and got in my face, no fear? She had no idea who I was or that I could wipe the floor with her in just a few seconds. She didn't care, just did her thing. I like her. You do too." Not a question, a statement. It's a true one, but no less confusing than when Eve was first dropped off by the horde in North Carolina. Here, however, there have been no sleepovers so far. In a way, I'm glad since it's always been a little confusing to me. Does she just want companionship and a warm body to sleep against for comfort? More? Somewhere in between? Eve usually just retreats with Amy to their cabin in the evenings and remains there. I know there's a connection between the two of us, but I don't know any more now than I did before how it's going to turn out. While I want to be with her, it has to be completely right, and I'm not going to be the one to prompt anything. I don't know exactly how she feels for me, and we must be sure we're safe before chancing anything deeper that could be torn away. I'll tell her about DeeDee when it's time, and whatever is supposed to happen after that will happen. She's here, Morgan's here, we're reasonably safe and on familiar ground, so all is good for now in my book.

***

However, "all is good" can sometimes be translated to "all is boring," which isn't a terrible thing considering the alternative. Without the routines of normal life to fill time, we have a lot of idle hours once the chores of gathering are completed for the day. Having additional bodies to help speeds the task along nicely. We restock the wood supply for next winter's preparation and scour the cabins and houses within a few miles for anything that's edible, useful to us, or dangerous to zombies. Eschewing any traps that may harm the dogs by accident, we build collection chutes of sorts in the woods to channel any invading waves toward the driveway so we'll only have one direction to be concerned about. The four of us who are not working on the car cut down hundreds of new growth saplings from the dense woods and spend weeks nailing those across larger trees like a split rail fence. We're trying to create enough of a barrier that the zombies will hopefully follow an opening versus charge through or climb over. By the time that's done, it's full summer, and we pass a lot of time enjoying the simple pleasures of youth: playing beanbag toss, darts, and whiffle ball, collecting berries—one for the bucket, one for the mouth—taking walks, and boating and swimming in the lake.

Amy absolutely loves the water, though she has never learned how to swim, so Morgan sets to teaching her.

Morgan's idea of teaching her is the hard way, of course. Eve and I sit on the retaining wall, dabbling our feet in the cool water, and watch as they paddle to the center of the lake in one of the canoes. Then, without warning, Morgan stands up, grabs Amy, tosses her into the water, and tells the kid to figure it out. After a good bit of shrieking and spluttering, Morgan gives her a hand, but only for a moment, and then paddles a few feet away. Amy promptly stops thinking and starts doing, dog-paddling toward the canoe and safety. Morgan keeps letting the boat drift gently so the girl gets a hundred yards of swimming success without realizing it. The lake is small enough that every part of it is in sight at all times, and from where we sit, we can see the enormous grin on Amy's face as Morgan hauls her out of the water and hugs her ...

And then promptly throws her back in with a huge smile of her own.

"Your sister," Eve says, with the bemused grin most people seem to have when observing Morgan from the safety of a distance, "is a *really* unique person. I hope you don't take that the wrong way, but I've never met anyone like her, with that strong of a personality. She's utterly fearless, isn't she? Not to mention how pretty and physically incredible she is. I bet growing up with her was fun most of the time."

"It was," I answer, taking no offense since Eve isn't exactly the first person who's made that kind of remark about Morgan, "and that's about right. 'Most of the time.' There was a lot of tension in the house when we hit our teenage years and Morgan began to run wild. My, *our*, parents didn't know what to do with her. She was always a phenomenal and, um, really competitive athlete, so that brought its own challenges. Then she started to grow more into her body, and the boys practically lined the street wanting to be near her, even ones five and six years older than her, which made our father nuts. And then you add in the fact that she knew exactly what was going on and would sneak out to go have fun, come home late, and so on, and there was always some kind of fuss. But the two of us—we were two peas in a pod. She covered my back, we played sports together endlessly, and she scared the shit out of every girl I dated and bawled a good few of them out when my feelings got hurt, which didn't exactly help my ego—not that she cared—but we were inseparable. I've missed her these last few years, warts and all. She's a good one to have on your team."

"Yeah, I can see that," Eve replies thoughtfully.

I look at her out of the corner of my eye, the sun high in the sky behind her. She's as pretty as before in a regular but not common way, her smooth skin still remarkably pale even after spending so much time outside. The brown hair that had been a short rat's nest when we first met is now neat and longer, reaching to the middle of her back and held together by a clawlike brown clip. I let my eyes drift over her delicate face without meaning to be seen and take in the pale but sensual lips, compact mouth, and petite nose. She's a complicated package herself, with an inside toughness that's belied by her visual vulnerability.

"What do you think about when you look at me like that?" she asks, startling and then embarrassing me since she was obviously aware of me watching her this whole time.

I redden and figure it's probably the right time to be honest. "I'm sorry, I don't mean to stare. That's rude."

"No, it's okay. I like the way you look at me, you've done it all along. I've just always wondered what you were thinking when you did, so I thought I'd finally ask you." Her voice is gentle and a bit softer than usual, and her eyes are fixed on mine.

I hesitate since I'm about to give a mixed message, and she may not like part of it. All the way back to when she first joined me, I've felt a contentment when she's near me. Not that we "belonged together" or some other trite movie term, but just a sense of peace and comfort in her presence. I decide to tell her that part first, conscious that when DeeDee and I had finally opened up, we were in almost exactly this kind of situation.

Hey, Romeo, shit or get off the pot. Say something stupid, or say something, stupid. Or both! You're looking at her again like a teenage girl who's mooning over one of those ridiculous sexy vampires. Yeah, you know the look.

I hate that voice sometimes, though it's usually right.

"Eve," I start, "I'm sorry, I don't mean it to seem like I'm staring at you. It's more just *looking* if there's a difference that makes any sense. I feel … I'm not sure how to put it … I feel right when I'm with you, and looking at you, studying you, is part of that. Like I'm supposed to be watching over you, caring for you, not because you need it or asked for it, but because I want to." I'm unsettled by not being able to explain how I feel, but I wasn't completely sure how to describe it to begin with. Not lust, though she is attractive. Not love since we don't really know each other well enough for that, and this world seems like a weird one for the old definition of "love," but something like partnership draws me to her strongly.

She sits and does some watching of her own, eyes fixed on me and looking at my face in an unselfconscious way, almost like the way small children look at the world—they don't know there are supposed to be barriers or rules, so they just look until they're done looking.

Eve is like that now and stays silent, though she's clearly thinking.

Eventually, she says, "You and DeeDee. You were together." Not a question.

I nod. There isn't anything that words will do better than a nod, though I'm a bit surprised she said it or even figured it out.

She nods herself. "Okay. I'm sorry," she says but then quickly catches herself and places a hand on my arm. "Not that you were together. That's completely fine. I kind of expected it. She was attracted to you, and she was attractive and well, DeeDee, so there was going to come a time when she'd act on her feelings. What I mean is I'm sorry she died. I'm sorry you were right there and couldn't help her or save her. I know that had to hurt, horribly. Losing all of them, almost all at once, and not being able to do anything about it. You like to protect, and you couldn't. I'm so sorry."

She leans toward me and puts her hands on either side of my face, holding it and my gaze in one of the most intimate moments of my life. "It's not your fault, none of it. You're good, everything about you is good. You take care of us, all of us. This group and the last."

I think she might kiss me, but she doesn't, just folds herself into my arms for a long, warm hug that feels just right. I feel a deep ache in my chest—for the moment, the loss, or all of the above, I'm not sure. It doesn't really matter. Guess there's a first time for everything. I've always wanted the girl to kiss me in the past, but I'm glad she didn't. There's still some sorting out to do about this. I've gone through my emotional life preferring to not do something if there was more chance of it going badly and being a crushing disappointment than being a success. This may not make sense to anyone else, but a couple of romances when I was young simply devastated me, and since then, I wouldn't allow myself to fall completely. My inside voice will probably call me a chicken, but a chicken that doesn't leave the farm doesn't get hurt.

Not true! Those chickens end up being dinner! And yeah, you're a chicken.

Quit it.

And, my emotions are still raw from losing everyone, especially after my short, closer connection with DeeDee. This version of the world is nasty that way—few moments of true happiness offset by too many moments of shocking and sudden brutality. I don't want to have this go awry. It's too important to risk it being anything other than just right.

We have to be safe; that's job number one, two, and three for me.

Neither of us notice Ned standing in the doorway to the garage a few dozen yards away, motionless and watching with a wrench in one hand and a greasy red rag in the other, before fading back into the shadows. Morgan, however, even from well offshore in the canoe, sees and notes.

***

We're always alert, always looking and listening, but we also have the dogs as an advantage since they'll smell any zombies well before we hear them, or, at least, they will if we're downwind. Things are pretty good—no monsters come to visit, and we all get along even though Ned's a touch on the outside due to his fascination with the car. Morgan and I handle the heavy patrolling duties, though, at times, Eve and I pair up or Morgan and Eve go for the run around the lake. One dog always stays back, which is a struggle at first since Ajax and Jack remain attached to me and Morgan, but they eventually start to understand the drill and the home dog will rest on the porch, head down on his paws and eyes scanning from side to side.

Eve is a superb athlete herself, and while she lacks the raw power of either me or Morgan, she has the force of will that makes the difference between jock and star. There are plenty of days where everyone will come home sweaty because the patrol turned into a competition, but that is solved by jumping in the lake to clean off and cool down.

Amy isn't much for physical contests, but she enjoys anything to do with marksmanship, like Amelie had. Maybe the past popularity of video games had its upside after all. While we haven't done any shooting with guns for the sake of keeping the noise down, she shows prodigious skill with darts, bean bags, and DeeDee's crossbow. Anything to do with fine touch and aim. She'll set dominoes, of all things, standing on edge on a tree stump and then picks them off from twenty paces or more. It makes a mess of the dominoes.

For his part, Ned continues to disassemble the car and inspects each piece, cleans it if needed, sets it to the side, and makes copious notes about what's in good order and what isn't. He's quiet in general when we all hang out, but he makes pleasant-enough conversation and usually perks up if we ask him what he's worked on that day even if most of the terminology sails clean over our heads. I'm hopeful he'll be able to get the car running, though, since like most everything else at the lake, it holds memories.

I'm always conscious of the group of zombies in town. Before Top, Amelie, and Mabel were ambushed and died, there had been about forty of them. The three of them killed roughly half of those, and I picked off a couple when trying to save Amelie, but twenty is still a big number when only two of us are going to fight the truly messy part of any fight. I don't think we can give Ned a rifle and expect him to do much damage based on his behavior when he arrived, and while Amy is a good shot at stationary targets, she's a kid and the horror of an actual moving target that's trying to kill and eat you will almost certainly unnerve her, so we can't plan on her as an asset in a brawl. And despite Eve's steel spine and competitive drive, I don't have a sense that she'll really be able to wade in and kill unless cornered. There's a gentleness to her nature that isn't all the way ready for all the hard parts of the world as it is now; she needs people like me and Morgan to take care of the dirty work. This is probably just the way Morgan likes it—her against the world with her little brother tagging along.

One morning, Morgan and I wait until everyone else is settled and armed with a clear escape plan—simple: run like hell—in case they're invaded while we're gone, and then we go to scout the town and take stock of its ghastly residents. We take the dogs with us to balance the odds as much as possible and give us an early warning system. We bring guns with us, though only handguns so they'll be easier to carry for the 10-mile round trip—everyone in the army knows running with a long gun is shitty business—plenty of ammunition, edged weapons—Morgan is really fond of the machete, and I carry the KNIFE as always—water, and Morgan's Bo. We aren't planning on starting anything unless we run into a small enough group to eliminate them safely and escape without being tracked. That's my biggest concern about the group, that they'll find us by scent or dumb luck when we aren't all together or in the middle of the night. They have to go, but I can't come up with a way to get them all at once, and so Morgan talks through ideas on the way there. She tries to bait me into a race there, but I tell her we'll be better suited saving any energy in case we run into trouble and need to haul ass. In typical Morgan fashion, she agrees but then demands a race back home. I agree to this since I've been sensing that she needs more physical outlets than she's been getting and is restless with being out of her previous exercise routines. Plus, I want to finally win one of these races—there's nothing wrong with my sense of competition either.

About midway there, Morgan suddenly says, "I don't trust him."

It takes me a second to realize it's about Ned. "What do you mean? Why not?"

"He's too quiet, and I don't think it's because he's a quiet person. I think it's because he's thinking," she replies.

Morgan, even though her focus over the years has mostly been on herself, is an observant and intuitive person who carefully studies other people through their body language and the way they move. She looks for anything that gives her a competitive advantage. Is there a hint of a limp that indicates limited quickness? Do they meet her gaze, or is there a nervous flick of their eyes to the side? Anything for an edge. To me, Ned seems essentially harmless. He works on the car, does a share of chores like everyone else, is polite enough, and seems to get along well with all of us.

Morgan continues. "He was watching you and Eve the other day, when you were talking down at the waterfront. I watched him watching the two of you, and the expression on his face was *not* a pleasant one when you were hugging. He obviously has feelings for her, but she has feelings for you, so you're a problem for him."

I think about that as well as Eve's history with Jack and the complexity of my relationship with her. I have always given people the benefit of the doubt and second chances by nature, though that had almost cost me more than once with Jack way back in North Carolina. But now, there are so few of us left, and without any evidence other than a sour look on Ned's face, I'm not prepared to do anything rash.

"I'm not sure I agree with you, but you've always had a better sense for people's true nature than I have, and I trust that. So what do we do? Just watch him? It's not like we can kick him out. Besides, I think that would upset Eve and Amy. He saved Amy from being alone, and Eve says that without the two of them to keep her company through the winter, she didn't think she'd have made it. We owe him something."

"We could test him," Morgan says with a bit of a predatory grin. "Or, rather, I could test him. He definitely likes her, but I could see if he's actually fixated on her or just a bit pent up."

"You don't mean *sleep* with him?" I ask in astonishment. Morgan may have been pent up herself, but Ned is very much not her type. The rules of the world have changed and all, but I highly doubt her preference for physically dominant men has changed.

"Ew, no! That's gross. What's wrong with you?" she punctuates with a firm jab to my shoulder. "I just meant dangle the goods a bit in front of him and see how he reacts. The old honey pot trick. If he starts to show interest in me, we're all good, if not, and I doubt this, we have a looming problem that should be solved before it becomes an actual problem."

"I don't know. Say he does show interest in you, assuming you're his type, and then you blow him off. Isn't that a new problem?"

"Brother of mine, I'm *everybody's* type," she says with a proud toss of her ponytailed hair. "I think giving him some eye candy from time to time will be enough if it redirects him from obsessing over you being in the way of him and Eve. Maybe I'm wrong about that, but do you have any better ideas?"

I don't. None of this feels right to me, but above everything else, I'm going to keep everyone as safe as I can, so I tell her I'll think about it. My mistakes with Jack in the past still haunt me since there had been more than one clear sign that he was trouble and I'd been too forgiving, which almost got me killed and Amelie raped. The world may have been a less complicated place than it used to be on some levels, but not on all of them.

On we jog toward the town.

***

We slow as we close in on the meadow that bridges the foot of the trail to the edges of the town. Mindful of the ambush the zombies had laid for Top and Amelie, and sure that they're one-trick ponies who will leave watchers ready in case we're dumb enough to come back that same route, we circle the fringes, looking through the budding undergrowth for any signs of them.

Nothing.

Veering off to the outskirts of the houses that make up the newest buildings in a slow- growing town, we dart from cover spot to cover spot, watching the dogs for any alerts. A long ten minutes of this—and still nothing in sight— brings us to a couple of blocks from the center. Larger homes from a forgotten heyday provide better concealment with mature shrubs, trees, and fences, and we finally stop at a blue Victorian that has a curved turret stretching three stories toward the sky and looks over the rooflines of the neighboring homes. It should give us a clear view. An anomaly here, but a welcome one that we creep into, clear the floors and reach the top to peer through faded lace curtains down into the open space of the main intersection.

Damn … my heart sinks sharply, and I hear Morgan's gasping intake of breath. While we were coming in and seeing no evidence that zombies are still around, I foolishly allowed myself to hope they've moved on elsewhere to find food. Maybe we'll be able to live in peace with nothing more to worry about than Ned supposedly having the hots for Eve. The sanctuary in the mountains will be precisely that, and we can go do something about the unwilling residents trapped in Marcus's fortress to the west when we're ready.

I was wrong.

They, too, are gathering. Twenty was the worst I've been prepared for, but there are more than that. Many more. Perhaps fifty of them gathered from who knows where and are mostly wandering in the aimless way they do when there's nothing to chase and eat.

"Shit," whispers Morgan. The dogs are with us in the room and I can feel their tension as well.

Shit is right. We're going to have to do something about the mass of misery out there in the streets, and it's going to take a lot more than a straight-up fight. I've been hoping their numbers would be about the same so we could simply pick the majority of them off from a distance with rifles and hunt down any remnants as needed. This is a group worthy of several trashcan bombs or something with similar destructive power, but as I watch, I notice that mixed among the wanderers are stationary pairs a few hundred yards out in each direction.

They've placed sentries.

We keep watching for another thirty minutes or so and see just the single alpha that Top had reported on before—a male one in banged-up blue jeans and a raggedly white Dream Theater T-shirt. He stands in the center of it all, wordlessly directing steady activity among his followers, including sending other trios out in every direction on obvious patrols of their area.

Double-shit.

No bringing the fight to them this time. Even though they managed to ambush and kill my friends, they have clearly also learned to defend themselves since the loss of half their number is significant. And then they've restocked on top of that.

Morgan and I call the dogs to us quietly and beat a cautious retreat back to the cabins, our mood far dimmer than it was on the jog here, so much so that Morgan doesn't bother reminding me we were supposed to race back. Somberly, we come up with, talk through, and discard ideas on the way for killing as many of them as possible without a direct fight, but we come up with nothing good.

When we arrive, we share the bad news with the rest of the group, whose faces fall as much as I'm sure ours did when we saw the horde. We spend most of the rest of the day moping around and planning on stepping up our patrol routines to ensure we won't be surprised. Ned, Eve, and Amy are similarly stumped for how to possibly eliminate them in one fell swoop. Dinner that night is a quiet affair.

CHAPTER 12

Despite our worries, the zombies leave us alone. We patrol constantly now, working in a semicircular pattern from the cabins. We prepare for evacuation if needed. One plan we come up with is to swim out into the lake—now that Amy has become part fish after Morgan's "lessons"—and across it to the far side. No way the zombies will think to circle the water and be waiting for us on the far side, which someone on foot can reach more quickly than a swimmer, and they don't do well in water that I've seen so far. The natural instinct to at least try and swim seems to have vanished along with their desire for anything but making people into happy meals, so that's our preferred escape plan. I also build a safe room of sorts beneath the main cabin, cutting a trap door in the family room—while nervously waiting for my grandmother to materialize and catch me making a mess of her floors—and then creating a walled-in shelter that measures about eight feet square and four feet high, with the walls embedded in the soil under the house and anchored to the floor. I reinforced that wood as well to withstand any battering or weight. A heavy sliding bolt that can be locked from inside completes it, but while whoever uses the space will be safe, they'll also be trapped and in utter darkness if the monsters are patient or slow to leave. Last ditch is a run around the lake to the far side and a different road that leads back to the west and in the opposite direction from the town where they'll be coming from. I hope we don't have to use any of the three, but I gain some comfort in being more prepared and having options so we don't have to think, just do.

And, and you have actual multiple plans that aren't as stupid as the one you used last time ... even if it worked. Remember? The boobie trap? It's a good thing you have smart people to help you this time around.

Amy's our chief food gatherer, with patience and a knack for bringing in as much fresh fruit as we can eat, which is a fantastic change from soup and other stuff in cans. Eve works with her so they're in a pair with one plucking berries and the other on alert, and then they will rotate.

Ned keeps working on the BMW, and one morning, there's an actual cough of the engine from the garage, followed by an enormous billow of black smoke out one of the bay doors and a loud *bang* and colorful cursing. He emerges shortly afterward, wiping oil off of his forehead and, of all things, smiling. "I'm close! I'm going to need to go find a new head gasket after that, which won't be easy. Is there a phone book somewhere in the house? I hope there's a place nearby I can drive to that might have been a parts supplier for old Beemers, though I can't imagine there was much call for that up here. If not, I actually have that and some other things I think I'll need back at my place in Pennsylvania. It'd only take me a few hours round trip."

We look in the compact secretary-type desk that's tucked into the corner off to the right of the fireplace, but we find only a very local phonebook about the size of a magazine, not a regional one. No luck with anywhere carrying BMW supplies, which isn't surprising, but Ned is unruffled and says he'll just go back to his home shop. His enthusiasm is contagious, and so I toss him the keys to the truck and wish him good luck. I'm not going to go with him, not with me having to watch over Eve and Amy, with Morgan getting ready to patrol the driveway and surrounding areas soon. He looks a bit crestfallen at the idea of going solo, but then he just walks out. I'm not too worried about him taking the truck and leaving us without that particular vehicle—we can find another if we have to.

I follow him out to the driveway, where we run into Eve and Morgan practicing with DeeDee's crossbow, making nasty puncture marks in some old wood shingles we've found. "Eve," he says, "I'm going back home for a bit. I need to pick up some parts for the car so I can finally get it running. Would you care to join me?"

"No, thanks," she replies, without turning away from sighting in her next target. Not a brushoff, just the reply of someone concentrating on the task at hand, but I watch Ned's face and see disappointment and a touch of anger flit across his features.

"Oh, the Corvette. Can I take that instead? I've been wanting to get my hands on one of these new ones," he queries to Morgan.

She just stares at him … no reply.

"Fine. Back later," he retorts, with no attempt at masking his mood. He climbs into the truck, fires it up, and spins the tires a bit in the loose dirt as he turns around and leaves, trailing a faint dusty cloud up the hill and out of sight. I watch him go, thinking about Morgan's intuition and decide she's probably right. He should be watched carefully. Eve takes no notice of any of it, just sends another bolt home into a shingle with a thick *thunk*.

***

Time passes slowly some days in our new world, not quite as slowly as the work day before vacation had in the past, but without the constant input of, well … everything, our days draw out, and I have no complaints about that. It's utterly peaceful here, so the days are a treasure to linger on like I had as a kid.

No one wears a watch anymore; all the batteries are dead, and windup watches have long become passé, so I keep track of time by nothing more scientific than good guesses. It's sometime in the early afternoon, and Ned has been gone for a few hours. Not long enough to get back to Lake Ariel and back, but at least enough time to finish the first half of the trip and some of the way back. It's completely silent aside from the bullfrogs that never seem to have nothing to say during the warm months.

I'm sitting on the front porch in the warm sunlight that trickles through the lakeside trees, disassembling and cleaning one of the pistols out of routine even though it hasn't been fired in a while, when I see motion through the shrubs near the front porch of the closest cabin. Ajax hasn't budged at my feet—even badass guard dogs can't help but conk out in sunny spots—so there doesn't seem to be anything to worry about. It's not Morgan, not big enough, plus she's still out patrolling. I know Amy is taking a nap— she announced that a short while ago after hours of picking berries and trudged off with heavy feet to the second cabin. A flicker of bright yellow fabric and pale skin breaks through, and Eve emerges on the natural stone pathway that leads to the waterfront space where we swim and bathe. She doesn't look in my direction, so I doubt she knows I'm there. I keep quiet and simply watch her like I enjoy doing, and I'm a bit startled to see her when she comes fully into view. She's wearing an extremely tiny yellow bikini that doesn't cover much more than the most important pieces … and barely that.

The top doesn't cover the entire swell of her breasts even though she's compact, and the string that wraps to tie in the back looks like it's made from fishing line it's so thin. I forgot how fit she is since she usually wears modest and practical clothes that hide her figure, but the muscles of her stomach are well-defined, as are those of her shoulders and thighs. The bikini bottom is just as microscopic, with a virtual ribbon of fabric barely three inches wide covering her front and back, leaving her hipbones and much of the cradle of her lower stomach strikingly visible and making it impossible for me to tear my eyes away. I have always looked at women differently than my friends—more so out of admiration and studying than in a whoa-look-at-the-boobs-on-that-one kind of way that would make me uncomfortable when a buddy would give me the old nudge and nod toward a pretty woman. I admire women in their forties who clearly work out and watch their diets, mentally congratulating them for their discipline. The younger crowd has it easy to carry a good figure, but I've always found my eyes drawn to those who have worked hard to improve themselves. Someone in good shape is pleasing to my eyes, and Eve is making my eyes very happy, though I feel self-conscious for staring at her. Nothing to be done about that now. I've been watching for too long to make my presence known without her realizing I've been eyeballing her, so I hold my silence and visually drink her in as she steps down into the water. She splashes some up on her arms and then over her shoulders, shivering as it drizzles down her back. Even at more than fifty feet away, I can easily see the dark circles of her nipples harden through the yellow fabric as the cold water wakes them up. I feel ever more guilty for staring at her like this, but I just can't help myself. I saw her naked after she'd been delivered to me by the zombies what feels like ages ago, but this is far, *far* more fascinating.

"Hey! I got the parts," comes Ned's voice from behind me, startling me badly.

If the gun had been put together, I probably would have shot him. I'm instantly furious, but not at him. I'd been so lost in staring at Eve that I missed a five thousand-plus-pound truck rolling into the parking area and the sound of Ned walking across gravel and onto the porch. What if it had been a pack of zombies, who can be fairly stealthy? "What the fuck, Ned? You scared me!" I say more sharply than I intended, trying to get my heart rate back to something normal. My hands are shaking.

He looks at me, then over my shoulder at the water where he obviously sees Eve.

No dummy, he must have connected the dots, but he doesn't say anything about it. "Just thought you'd want to know I got them. It's maybe another couple of hours to take the head off and replace the gasket, and then it'll be ready for the road again." His flat eyes stray back over my shoulder again—can't blame him for that.

Without another word, he walks past me and down to the water and Eve, and I assume he will share the same good news about the parts. His back is to me as he stops to speak with her, and while I can't hear what they're saying, I keep watching.

***

Eve hears him coming and looks up, suddenly aware that he isn't whom she expected. She'd been completely cognizant of what she was doing and that she was being watched—women always know when they're being watched, just rarely choose to acknowledge it. Ned's arrival startles her, however, and she's immediately uncomfortable. She's scarcely clad in the swimsuit and obviously chilly. Also, she's standing two steps below Ned, so she doesn't like that submissive position. Feeling foolish now and very self-conscious, she makes eye contact with Ned and mentally dares his eyes to wander, but she knows she's going to lose that challenge.

He doesn't disappoint; his gaze hungrily takes her in, all of her, as he stands there and says nothing at first. Seconds tick by and her discomfort increases. He's standing between her and the safety of the towel sitting on the green-and-black bench, and she feels herself getting even cooler as the sun ducks behind an unwelcome cloud, but she doesn't want to let him know he's making her uncomfortable.

Finally, after at least a minute of being visually molested, she relents and crosses her arms across her chest. Ned clearly doesn't give a crap and drops his gaze shamelessly to her pelvis, unwavering. Eve is angry now and embarrassed and a little frightened. She goes to move to the side and get out of the water, but Ned steps sideways, too, and as he does so, she catches sight of his prodigious erection.

Oh no, she thinks, her fear increasing. She knows nothing is going to happen, not here, not now with others around, but her mind flips back to the episode with Jack in the bathroom on New Year's Eve those years ago, which spurs her into movement. This time, she steps to the side and out of the water, not caring that she brushes against him—though, thankfully, not *that* part of him—as she makes her way to the towel and modesty. "What do you want, Ned?" she asks as she wraps the towel around her, trying to hide her fear and also wanting to quietly handle this herself.

"Isn't that obvious?" he replies with something of a smirk and glances down at his torso. "I want you. I told you that back in Pennsylvania. I wanted to stay there, just us, but *no*, you wanted to come here and be with him. Did you know he was eye fucking you just now while you were prancing around for him like a ... a hooker in that suit? It's okay for him to look, but not me? You don't even know if he likes you like I do. I would have always been there for you, but you decided to put on your little peacock display while I was gone. I see the truth now, and clearly."

Eve has seen people angry before but not like this. His words pummel her, but they are delivered in a low, flat monotone she knows won't carry up to the porch. She pulls the towel tighter around her, but she feels her own indignation rising. "Ned, stop it. You're making me really uncomfortable. I'm leaving." She moves to go around him and head back to the cabin.

"Not so fast," he rasps, his arm snaking out to grab hers in a surprisingly strong grip and stopping her from getting past him. "Where do you think you're going? I'm not done talking ...." He stops abruptly as he hears the sound of a chair scuttling across the wooden surface of the porch, but he doesn't let go immediately and holds her eyes for a moment longer. "Whore." He then finally drops her arm and walks off along the shoreline back toward the garage without looking up at the porch.

Eve has never been so upset or so humiliated in her life. Not when it became obvious divorce was the best option; not when the goddamn zombies took over the world and she had to hide for days, starving and thirsty and terrified; not when that asshole Jack had tried to force himself on her; and not when her father died. All she wanted was a respite from what life had been like for the past year. After all this time of bundling up and covering herself in layers of clothing, of feeling like she needs to hide her body out of modesty or fear, she wanted to feel attractive, knowing she's safe here.

Ned's coarse words and judgment shattered that and made her feel cheap. Without looking up at the porch herself, she scampers to the darkness of her cabin, drops the towel on the floor, strips off the wet suit, throws it angrily into the corner, lies down next to Amy's slumbering form, and quietly cries until she falls asleep.

***

I couldn't hear the exchange between Eve and Ned since his back had been to me the whole time and they both spoke quietly. But I don't need to be an expert in reading body language to understand what went on. Eve's had been awfully easy to follow, and I didn't like it at all when Ned grabbed her arm, and I stood up when he did. That seemed to defuse things, or at least, bring them to an end, but I'm still not pleased. Part of me wants to go check on Eve, part of me wants to go confront Ned and maybe push him around a little—or maybe a lot—but I decide to wait. I want to talk with Morgan when she comes back in from her patrol. It looks like she's completely right with her concerns, and I don't want to repeat the mistakes of the past, but he's one of the few humans left, and I just can't justify killing a man—grabbing a woman's arm isn't a capital crime, even now.

You got damn lucky with Jack, if you'll recall. That was over a girl, too, and almost got you killed because you're too nice for your own good. But it's not only about you, and what if no one is lucky this time? Now you can't leave them alone together. Maybe you can't leave him with Amy either. Let your big sister handle this. She won't hesitate at all. For a chick, she's got a serious set of balls, where yours seem to shrink up when it's time for dirty work with people.

At least you keep them in place when it's zombie-killing time, I'll give you that.

***

Morgan arrives back from her patrol an hour or so later, Jack in tow and both of them sweaty messes. After greeting me, she steps into the main cabin and emerges shortly after in her own "swimsuit," which consists only of underwear and a white T-shirt. I know immediately where this is going and try to stop her, but she bounds past me off the porch, down onto the path, and plunges in a shallow dive into the still water of the lake.

After a good thirty seconds, she comes into view well offshore and whistles for the dogs. Ajax and Jack wallop the water like a couple of pontoons dropped from a height and wade around with goofy grins on their faces, lapping up as much as they can stomach, and then they clamber out and shake in wild sprays of water and dog spit. They remain nearby, barking happily for no reason whatsoever.

I grin at the racket and walk down to the water myself, not intending to swim but just to get a recap of her patrol. Morgan swims on the surface on her way back in, with smooth, strong strokes that quickly bring her to the shallows where she can stand up. Decades of playing sports and training for them when she wasn't playing left her with a phenomenal physique that balances femininity and ferocity. Muscles ripple everywhere under her skin as she washes herself modestly with her back to me. Not a shred of fat on her frame, and her back falls in a sharp V from shoulders to waist, and then she flares only a bit at the hips. We chat idly, nothing to report from her run, no creatures stirring nearby.

I'm watching Jack lean down toward the water for more to drink when Ajax perks his head toward the garage. I swing my head around to see what has caught his attention.

It's just Ned standing in the dark doorway and silently watching the fracas at the waterfront with a blank expression. When he sees me turn around, he withdraws without a change in expression or a glance toward the siren taking a bath in practically nothing.

Yup ... we have a problem.

I don't want to risk talking to Morgan right now about what I saw earlier on the chances we could be overheard—and in case my impulsive sister acts like ... well, my impulsive sister. I also have a new problem: I now don't want to leave Eve alone with Ned, especially without getting Morgan up to speed first. Finally, I decide we'll take a quick patrol together tomorrow and simply circle the lake while I fill her in on the news.

That night is an unsettled one. All of us eat together as we typically do, but it's a near silent meal. Both Amy and Morgan look around the table with mild curiosity on their faces. Eve eats quickly and excuses herself without explanation. I catch a raised eyebrow from my sister, but I just shake my head. Everyone goes to bed in their normal quarters, which I'm not wild about; but I figure if anything happens, it'll be noisy, and I'll be in the second cabin in moments.

It still takes me a long time to go to sleep. I lie there for what feels like half the night, listening to the soothing wheeze of Ajax sleeping off his active day, and finally drift away myself after a lot of internal turmoil that gives me no answers.

CHAPTER 13

The next day blares to life with a clear, cool morning that's typical for summertime in that neck of the woods. I can see my breath as I stand over the grill and heat water for coffee. I miss cream and sugar, and while there's enough powdered creamer left in the world for the rest of my life, I really don't like that; nor do I like sugar-only coffee, and so I have finally eschewed both and drink it black. Amy even drinks a bit despite her youth though she complains it isn't as good as Starbucks. Sigh. I can't even say "kids these days" since there's just one of them. It's barely still coffee by the time those Starbucks baristas are done doctoring it up with caramel this and whipped that, but whatever. Just another "problem" solved by the eclipse of humanity's rule of the planet.

I figure I'm the only one up until I hear a starter motor spin, then a snort of the BMW's engine, followed by the engine revving, nearly stalling, revving again, and then settling into a mostly smooth idle. Clouds of bluish-gray smoke erupt from every door and window of the garage pursued by a whoop of triumph. Since the opening for cars is on the far side of the building and out of my sight line, I walk around the side with my mug in hand to see what's happening.

Ned's just backing the car out and stops to roll the window down with an enormous smile on his face that makes me forget the conflict at the waterfront yesterday. "I did it! I got this baby running. Listen to her purr. I did it, dammit. I did it!" His face is lit by the happiness that hits every car guy's face and makes him look like a kid again. "I'm going to take her out for a spin. I guess if I'm not back in about thirty minutes, come find me. I'll go east when I hit the main road."

"Okay, but go west instead of east, so turn left. East is where the zombies are hanging out, and you don't want to run into them. Nice job." The last bit feels trite, but I have to admit that I'm pleased that he's gotten the car running and really don't want him to be a problem I have to solve in a violent way. Besides, some encouragement costs me nothing at all.

"Good point. Okay, here we go! Back in a bit, I hope."

I watch him back the dusty, white car around and hold my breath as it nearly stalls before catching and roaring—in a fairly sedate, BMW kind of way—up the driveway, morning sunlight winking off the chrome bumpers and trim as it vanishes into the shadows of the heavy tree canopy.

***

Ned's success with the car solves my problem of how to talk to Morgan in private. I wander back to the main cabin, step over Jack, who's still slumbering deeply beside her, and rouse her carefully. For a woman as beautiful as she is, Morgan can look rather hilarious in the morning. It must be a product of her ever-busy mind even when sleeping, but she wakes each morning with her hair standing in every direction. This morning is no different, with strands shooting in a helter-skelter pattern across the pillow and a spectacular mohawk standing at attention in the middle.

"Whatdayawant?" she mumbles incoherently and rolls over, hiding her head beneath the pillow.

It's still early, after all, and she took a very long route yesterday and has to be worn out. But we have thirty minutes or so before Ned returns, so this needs to be quick. I walk into the kitchen and grab a second mug of coffee, handing it to her when I return and explaining what I saw.

"I'll kill him," she says, so matter-of-fact that I'm not sure if she's kidding or not.

I disagree. "No, we can't do that. He's a human, and we don't know exactly what happened other than he was upset with Eve. We can kill *them*, but not us."

"Really? Are you just dense or so committed to saving everyone that you'd pick him over her? That's what you're doing. Besides being attracted to her, he feels like she owes him something for watching her throughout the winter. We talked about this. He's completely nuts about her, and the two of you have … whatever it is you have going on, and he sees it. That's eating at him. You know it, I know it, and it's just a matter of time. He laid hands on her. It'll only escalate from here. I know about these things. He has to go."

Stung by the rebuke and her impeccable logic, I reluctantly agree. Not to kill him though. I can't condone that even though, as we talk, Morgan volunteers to take him on a patrol, take care of business, and come back. That'll just make me feel guilty. So we finally agree that we'll tell him he has to leave. We'll give him supplies—no weapons in case that backfires—and let him have his pick of vehicles.

The European thrum of the BMW's engine carries down the driveway a few minutes later, signaling Ned's return and bringing back memories of hearing the same sound when my grandfather returned from errands many years ago. We haven't talked about when we'll expel him, but in typical Morgan fashion, she hops out of bed, tosses a sweatshirt over her tank top, and marches out the door, saying over her shoulder, "No time like the present!"

We run into Eve on the front porch, who's looking groggy herself. Wordlessly, she follows us to the gritty surface of the driveway and the idling car. Ned is smiling in the blue driver's seat, running his hands over the surfaces of the interior in what looks like wonder. He doesn't hear our approach at first, but then he turns to look at us, the smile fading from his face as he does so. He knows something is coming, just not what, and knows it isn't going to be good. Like a parent nudging their child to do something that makes them nervous but is a good lesson in life, Morgan stands silently and looks at me with an expression that says, "Well?" on her face. Dammit. I have to do the dirty work.

About time, Sally.

You, I don't need right now.

"Ned …." I start, then catch myself almost saying, *We're voting you off the island*. I continue as he climbs out of the car. "You have to leave. We'll give you more than enough food and water to keep you stocked for a while, and you can take whatever vehicle you want, even the Corvette." I have the pistol tucked into the back of my shorts as always, but I'm not going to bring it out unless needed.

His face darkens into an expression of loathing, and he stares at Eve as if trying to injure her with his eyes alone. It looks like there's an internal battle raging within him, and for a moment, I think he's going to blindly attack. I slip my hand around to grasp the pistol's grip. For a fairly mild-mannered and ordinary-looking man, the change is startling.

He never breaks eye contact with Eve as he says, "So you ran off to tattle to your *savior*, did you? He'll always save you—is that it?" he spews, the anger setting his eyes afire. "I *protected* you, I *watched* over you through the winter, I took *care* of you and Amy and brought you here, and this is the thanks I get. You'd be dead without me. I should have left you alone, such a pathetic sight you were, dragging the corpse of your father through the snow. Amy and I would have been fine. We didn't *need* you. Dead. You'd be dead. It would be better if you were *dead*!"

At this, Morgan steps in front of him, forcing him to break both his raging diatribe and eye contact with Eve, who's slid slowly behind me, gasping as his words cut into her. Before Morgan can say or do whatever she has in mind, he bores into her. "And *you*. You think you're better than everyone. Prettier, stronger, tougher, smarter. You're a whore too! I saw you displaying yourself yesterday, to your precious brother no less. Whores! All whores! I don't need anything from you, but I'm taking *my* car, this one. Go get Amy, bitch. We're leaving."

Like a shuffling deck of cards, I step between Morgan and Ned. I can see she's boiling over, and while she could likely beat the shit out of him even on his best day, this needs to end now. I'm shaking with anger myself. We gave him a chance to accept this quietly, but that obviously isn't going to work. I have to finish it, so I do. I bring the pistol out, jam it roughly under his chin, and push him back toward the car. "That's not happening. Amy is staying here with us, where she's safe. Final answer. Get the fuck out before I shoot you right here. This is over."

He looks at me with the same anger as with Eve, and a part of me wants him to try something so I can vent my own anger. Morgan can beat him with tactics and skill. I outweigh him by at least thirty pounds of muscle, and I would beat him with savagery and brute force. I feel myself leaning farther in and getting ready to drop the gun when I feel a gentle hand on my arm.

Eve. "Don't," she says softly.

And that's it.

Ned turns, gets back into the car, and reverses up the driveway without looking at any of us again.

The three of us watch him go. Eve is the first to leave, quietly and without a backward glance. I want to go and talk to her, comfort her, but as I step to follow, my sister reaches out her own hand. "Don't. Not now."

***

It's a weird day, which makes for two in a row. Morgan simmers for hours after Ned drives away, not having a good outlet for her own anger. She paces back and forth through the property, spinning the Bo in a series of intricate moves that make it look like a brown, blurring circle. Eve has retreated back to her cabin, from which Amy emerges a couple of hours later. She asks where Ned is, and I simply tell her that he left and is gone for good. That garners nothing more than a noncommittal shrug from the teenager, then she ambles off to read in the hammock attached to two of the towering hemlocks that loom between the main cabin and garage.

I fume. I don't feel any guilt at telling him to leave, not after that confrontation in the driveway. He's clearly off his rocker, and I believe we did the right thing even if it had been a disturbing and miserable few minutes. I wanted to defend my sister, my friend, and myself from the accusations he'd thrown around like rice at a wedding. But what I really wanted was a fight. It's been a while since we've had any kind of brawl, and I realize I have gotten used to the conflicts with the zombies and the utter freedom they provide. To act and kill without remorse or hesitation is a horribly alluring thing.

I should be careful what I wish for …

Because I'm going to get it.

CHAPTER 14

It's late afternoon, with the descending sun perhaps an hour away from brushing the distant tree line beyond the lake's far shore. Morgan and I have been sitting, cleaning all our weapons out of weekly routine, and talking again about how to wear down the population of zombies in town. The plan so far is to show ourselves to small groups, lead them on a chase away from the town, and then kill the pack with as little risk as possible. We'll all go so we don't have to worry about Amy and Eve being alone, we'll take the truck instead of running there to preserve our legs, and we'll use rifles to eliminate the bulk of them from a distance where we can. The thought is that this will enable us to kill most of them over the next few weeks, then we can sweep the town in the same way they have to eliminate any remnants. And then, we will truly have peace.

No zombies, no Ned, no tension.

No such luck.

The same thrum of the BMW's engine sounds from up the driveway, and Morgan and I look at each other in confusion and a little bit of alarm. Ajax gives a short, sharp bark and rises to his feet.

Ned's back? Why?

We scoop up weapons—me with the pistols I've been cleaning and Morgan with the Bo and crossbow—and trot to the driveway, trailed by the dogs. This time, I can tell the car's coming back more slowly, and before any part of it comes into view, Eve and Amy, summoned by the sounds, drift up behind us with their fruit-gathering containers in hand. I see winks and twinkles of the car as it reaches parts of the driveway where the overhead foliage is thinner than in other spots. I also see motion that isn't an automobile, but I can't make it out clearly. I can just tell it's a lot of motion.

As you face the cabins from the water, the driveway is to the right, and the foot of the driveway in front of the garage is about twenty feet lower than the parts leading from the main road. A short, steep slope brings you down to basically water-level at the last moment, and so anyone who stops before that slope has the high ground.

Anyone … or any*thing*.

In any good western movie, there's always a scene in which a line of Indians on horseback stand, fanned out and impressive in number, atop a rise. Shuffling into view in the same manner is what looks like the entire population of the town, with my grandfather's BMW puttering along slowly in the middle and then coming to a halt at the top of the hill.

All the fucking zombies … led here by Ned.

Looks like you should have killed him when you had a chance, sunshine. You're in a shitload of trouble this time. I got nothing

else. Captain Obvious is signing off. I want no part of this one.
Come get me when this is over ... if you can.

Most of them are far enough away from the car that
Ned can open the driver's door and stand partly out of the
car. The four of us stare in shock at the number of zombies
and the terrible disadvantage we're at. Only partly armed,
occupying the low ground, ambushed. The two dogs stand
their ground, growling low in their throats and ready to
go. I feel adrenaline pound through my body as I scan the
monsters above us and decide what to do next. I'm not going
to panic; there's no point in that. I'm going to analyze and
count. I see the alpha, plus at least one of everything else—
young, old, male, female, large, and small.

Run, all of us? We need to go toward the main cabin to
grab more weapons from the tables on the porch and maybe
to stash Eve and Amy in the safe room under the floor if we
have time.

Standing and fighting here is a terrible strategy, and I'm
edging backward when Ned speaks to me directly this time.
"I'm back, savior. Can you save her this time? I think not!
I brought them, *all of them*. Eve! There you are, dear. Did
you miss me? Did you fuck him today after I left, or are
you going to wait a day or two? If I can't have you, bitch,
no one will. Except as *food*!" He cackles wildly and hops up
and down as he does so, barely containing the madness that
has led him to betray his own kind to the abominations that
have overrun the world.

Morgan's the first to react, bringing the crossbow
up quickly, sighting, and pulling the trigger in a blur of

continuous motion. Crossbows are nasty weapons, capable of firing a bolt well over three hundred fifty feet per second, and their bolts are even less pleasant, especially the broadhead type that are basically three-prong razor blades attached to the shaft that will spin and shred on impact. It's not three hundred feet from us to the car, so in less than one second, Ned goes from howling in triumph at the top of his lungs to staring at the arrow that has gone clean through the pristine metal of the driver's door of the car and his left leg, pinning him to the car. He shrieks, first from the pain of the penetration and then when he tries to extricate his leg from the cruel barbs jutting from the back of his thigh. But he doesn't cry for long. Zombies do like the smell of blood, and those nearest him fall on him like locusts, biting and tearing until the screaming stops.

Muuuuuuuhhhhh!

"Run!"

All six of us race back toward the main cabin. Dogs may not understand English, but they take the we-need-to-get-the-fuck-out-of-here hint. Our lead on the horde is maybe thirty yards, and we gain a precious second or two by moving first before they begin to pour down the driveway in a grabbing, pushing, caterwauling river of the ravenous dead.

"Eve, you and Amy into the safe room, now!" I shout as we reach the cabin and fly onto the porch at top speed. I grab the shotgun from where it's propped against a rocking chair, rack it to chamber a round, and begin to pour fire into the lead zombies as the two women pound inside and flip open the hatch. Morgan stays at ground level and fires two more shots from the crossbow, but they don't do much to bodies that can't, or don't, feel pain, so she quickly casts the crossbow to the side with a yell of frustration and hauls out her own pistol.

Once Morgan and I hear the hatch bang shut, we start running away from the mob, grabbing what weapons and ammunition we can from the tables, and then settle into a trot just faster than the zombies typically manage. They follow us in a shambling parade of jogging corpses through the sparse grass that leads to the woods in the near distance and funnel onto the path around the lake.

"We need to do what we were just talking about," Morgan says as we reach the fringes of the trees. "Draw them to us, kill some, and keep moving. We've just got to kill them all, today. Up for the challenge?"

I turn toward her and can't believe it. She's actually smiling. There are forty or more zombies chasing us, we have two people, two dogs (albeit badass ones), and a handful of weapons, and she's enjoying herself *and* turning it into a competition. Only Morgan can do that, but there's no one I'd rather have at my side even if this is going to be the end. I nod and smile back.

We spend the next twenty minutes jogging ahead of the pack, stopping after building a bit of a cushion to pick a few of them off, running ahead again while changing clips or reloading shells to the shotguns, and repeating it until there's a breadcrumb-like trail of the newly re-dead littered in our wake. We eventually reach the shooting range on the far side of the lake, which is an open area around the size of a football field, dotted with blueberry and other small shrubs coming no further up than midthigh. I'm out of shells and down to whatever's left in the last clip in the .45 plus the KNIFE, and I hear Morgan's own shotgun click empty as we broach the tree line edging the range.

"I'm almost out too," I tell her. "Think we've got to do the rest of this the hard way."

There are a dozen of them left, and some of those are injured and hopping or dragging themselves along on stumps, doggedly pursuing us.

"Okay," she says, "here seems right anyway."

We toss the shotguns to the side, check the remaining ammo in our pistols, and get ready. The dogs coast to a stop as we do, and we form our own battle line. I'm glad the dogs are on our side as they bristle in readiness for their part of the conflict and then tear across the open space in black and brown blurs to engage the monsters at the ends of the line, their challenging bellows sending primordial shivers down my spine. The fight is going to be longer and harder than I would have liked since the odds still aren't great even though we picked off a good number on the flight. All I have remaining is the KNIFE and three rounds, while Morgan has her machete and two rounds, so we let them close in on us enough to make the most of our ammunition, though Morgan misses with a shot. I'll make sure to remind her about it later, if there is a later.

There are eight zombies remaining now, and once they see us drop the firearms, they speed their approach even more, howling that goddamn howl as they come. It's messy, bloody work. Going inside arm's reach with the zombies is always risky since they're stunningly powerful, thanks to the unending hunger that drives them relentlessly, heedless of injury or pain. I spin and slash at necks and other limbs, whatever is nearby, and keep moving. Morgan, too, carves her own path through the sickening army of darkness, removing heads with surgical, savage swipes of the machete. Blood splashes everywhere, but none of it is ours. When I pause at one point, confronted by a pair and deciding which one to go after, I see Ajax flying from behind the one on the left. The dog hurls himself into the zombie's legs, knocking it down, and then dives his pumpkin-sized head into the neck, tearing away in a wrenching move and spraying viscera in a bloody circle. I'm *really* glad the dogs are on our side.

At the end, I think we're in trouble, surrounded by the last four and turned back-to-back, but the dogs barrel into the flanks again and peel off two of them to allow us the space to finish off the others. Morgan dispatches one quickly with a downward-angled strike of her blade that nearly severs its left arm and shoulder completely from the torso, and then she finishes it with a backhanded swipe that leaves a guttering stump where the head used to be. The final one rushes me in a flailing attack, arms pounding about my head and shoulders in heavy blows that stagger me. I fight to keep my balance and deflect its battering limbs away from my face. At last, I get an opening and drive the KNIFE into its forehead to the hilt. You can't do that to a human, the blade would skid off the bone, but the slight softness of zombie

bones doesn't provide such armor, and the monster falls in a heap at my feet.

It has been no more than a half hour since they arrived, but we're a sweaty, blood-spattered mess from head to toe. The dogs are lathered in sweat and the blood of their conquests, but while both of them have their tongues hanging well out of their mouths, they look happy in the way that only dogs can. Fatigue washes over me as the adrenaline coursing through my veins abates, and I sink to one knee and watch sweat and blood drizzle off my hair, arms, and everything else to fall into the trampled grass. I can see Morgan is in the same boat, though still grinning. Her sweatshirt is torn and missing a sleeve, and blood spray decorates most of her exposed skin and remaining clothes. We're pretty damn gross, but we're still standing.

"We did it."

"We need to go back."

"Yeah. Wanna race?"

I just shake my head.

I place one foot on the chest of the one I just killed and yank the KNIFE out, flinging a bloody spray of something nasty across the nearby grass. Surveying the bodies scattered around us to make sure there are no creatures stirring, we pick up the shotguns and pistols we dropped and go back the way we'd come, pausing at each cluster of bodies to confirm they're all really dead. We find a few of them dragging themselves down the path, missing a piece of a leg or an arm, weakly moaning and trailing gore in their wake. We cut their heads off with the machete and keep moving.

***

The safe room is dark, an ebony-clad space beneath the floor of the cabin. It smells strongly of the soil that has been disturbed to make it deep enough to hold people and of the sawdust from cutting the planks and supports. As soon as Eve and Amy tuck themselves under the hatch and slam it shut, Eve finds the sliding bolt by touch and shoots it home with a satisfying *clank*. There's also a support post made of a pair of two-by-fours nailed together to provide vertical strength against anything standing on the hatch itself, and she quickly props it under the center.

The two of them huddle together off to the side, trying to make themselves as small as possible. Eve holds Amy tightly against her for comfort—for both of them, she quickly realizes—and they go silent, scarcely daring to breathe. They hear the noises of the stampede of monsters following across and around the porch and then nothing for a minute, then two, then three. Several more minutes pass, and Eve feels herself beginning to relax but shuddering at whether they're going to get out of this mess and from Ned's actions and words. Her thoughts run wild in the dark. How could he betray them like that? She never led him on, never lied to him, yet, somehow, all of it combined into his unspeakable behavior. Surely, the swimsuit alone hadn't prompted him to ….

A sound.

The sound of a tentative footstep on the wooden surface of the porch.

She feels Amy take a breath and knows she's about to say something, so she claps her hand over the child's mouth and then uses her hand to shake Amy's head gently from side to side. Amy tenses and then nods. She gets it.

Another step … and then a few more. They're inside the cabin, and Eve feels her gut turn deeply cold with terror. The steps move closer and closer until she knows they're right above them, standing on the hatch door itself and then stopping.

More silence.

The impact is abrupt and shocking as the frame of their safe space is rocked with the blow, and the hatch door bounces a bit in its frame, allowing a sliver of light to enter for a split second. Something heavy has landed on the hatch, and Eve guesses one has jumped into the air and then landed with all its weight in an attempt to shatter the boards.

It knows they're down here.

The sinking feeling increases, and they clutch one another in the darkness, praying to something, anything, for safety.

Another jump and *thud*, but the door holds as the latch bolt rattles in its steel eye, and she hears small fragments of something loosen from the blow and fall onto the dirt. Amy lets out a small scream, and Eve fights to control her own panic, trying to be strong for the child. She's certain they're going to be ripped out of the space and eaten alive, and she wishes she had grabbed one of the guns on her way in to end it on her own terms. Anything is better than being savaged by the monstrous beings above them. But it's too late. All they can do now is hold each other, hold on and hope.

Silence again, and then a terrible, manic scrabbling like that of a dog's claws digging in wood, though she knows those are human nails. More and more join in, and she can hear the fibers of the wood shredding slowly and the grunts of effort from their attackers. Eve isn't sure if it's better to be completely in the dark until they're torn loose or if seeing the assault would be preferable, but she feels her mind starting to slide as her fear becomes too much to bear.

Insanity would be better; anything would be better than this … this slow march toward death.

She closes her eyes, though it makes no difference in the depths of their trap. Finally losing her faint grip on control and sanity, she joins Amy and screams her throat ragged in terror.

But somehow, the door holds.

The zombies tear at it for a few more moments, and then they suddenly quit. Quiet footsteps lead away in several directions, and then all is silent.

They wait …

Are they gone? Eve wonders. *Are the siblings coming back? Are they dead?*

And wait.

***

Out of subconscious habit, I pick up a spare full clip for the pistol and pop it in as we reach the steps leading up to the porch. In the haste of our flight, we'd only gathered what we could as we ran, and ammunition is scattered across the green planks, chairs, and the sparse grass adjacent to the stone steps.

Morgan packs a few shells into her shotgun as she ascends the steps silently. We think we've gotten them all, we can't be sure. The front door stands ajar, and I can't remember if it had been closed when we ran. I peer through the windows of the eating area and see nothing, and the hatch is intact and in place on the floor, so we go inside.

I crouch down on one knee and knock lightly on the wooden surface, which is wildly gouged by dozens of fresh scratches. "Eve?" I ask quietly. "It's us. It's me. You can come out. It's safe."

Stifled sobs greet me from the floor, followed by scuttling noises and the rattling click of the bolt being freed. The door opens a couple of inches, and I slip my fingers underneath to help with the weight and raise it open.

I hear only a single step before I'm mashed to the floor in a sprawling heap by the body that lands on my back. The small alcove between the family room and bedroom is dark and only a pace or two from where I've been crouched.

It's where he was hiding and waiting.

The alpha flattens me to the floor, my arms above my head, and I'm unable to get them underneath me to loosen him. The alpha who now grasps me with arms like steel bands from behind in a horrible, clasping mockery of an embrace. He sinks his teeth into my shoulder.

I've been bitten.

The pain of the bite is terrible and deep. I've never felt something like this in all my years, not even these most recent ones when I got cut and scraped during my many battles with the hordes of monsters. Not when I separated the same shoulder in a drunken spill during a college spring break, or when I broke my other arm falling off a ladder from twenty feet up. It's horrible, and I feel the skin tear raggedly as he rakes his head backward with a mouthful of my shirt and flesh. I'm helpless, down on the floor with his full weight on my back, and I can't shed him. I have no leverage. For the first time since all of this happened, I feel true fear. I think I'm going to die, right here.

The thunder of the shotgun blast shakes the walls of the cabin and echoes in the enclosed space. I feel small, hot pellets burn their way into my neck and back, and I'm flipped over as the zombie's head disappears in a fugue of crimson mist and his body lands with a *thump* in the same doorway he came from. I raise my eyes to see Morgan sighting down the barrel of her shotgun and then stagger to my feet. She fired from four feet away, taking the chance that she'd miss me enough. I'm deafened by the gun, in agony from the bite, and scared witless.

I've been bitten ….

CHAPTER 15

We drag the very dead, headless body out of the house and toss it down onto the ground aside the porch. There's going to be some serious cleanup needed after this battle. The question is whether I'm going to help with it or be part of what needs to be cleaned up. All of us and the dogs sit on the same porch while Eve ministers to my injury. There's no regular alcohol in the house, like rubbing alcohol, so in addition to the tall glass of Old Granddad I'm drinking to help with the pain, she pours most of the bottle over the torn skin. I howl as it sears my damaged flesh, and even once bandaged, it feels scarcely better.

I've been bitten.

I'm terrified, perhaps for the first time in my life. I've felt fear before, many times, but through all the fighting, the running, *this*—I've never been bitten. It's my greatest fear. Am I going to turn? Will I be aware of the change if I do, my mind slipping slowly from rational thought to madness until all I want to do is kill?

All three of the women sit wordless and miserable. I've handed over my weapons—we can't take the risk. For a moment, I consider telling them to shoot me, spare me what's surely coming, but one glance around the porch and I know none of them could do so before ... before I change. "Morgan, it's going to have to be you," I say. "When I change, you have to kill me. Just make it quick."

She raises her eyes to meet mine and shakes her head. "I can't kill my own brother. I'd rather shoot myself first," she replies with the steel in her voice that proves she means it. "You're the only one who's ever been there for me, always. I can't ... not you."

Eve then. I turn to her, but she speaks first. "No, I can't. It's the same as my father and mother ...." She raises a hand to her mouth, eyes wide, clearly recalling something. "No," she repeats. "Anything but that. I need you."

I need you.

The most powerful three words in the world, in any language, at any time.

I slide the safety off my pistol and hand the gun to Eve. She tries to push it away, but I hold her hands firmly and look deep into her eyes. "You have to. You have to protect the others if I change. You have to go on."

She stares back at me with her soft brown eyes filled with tears, but she doesn't break contact and finally gives an almost imperceptible nod.

***

And so I sit on the front porch of what I've always thought of as my grandparents' cabin that overlooks the small mountain lake. My shotgun rests outside of arm's reach against the dark wooden railing, and one of my well-used .45s is on Eve's right thigh in case she needs to shoot me in the face. I've got a tumbler of Old Granddad 100-proof whiskey close at hand, though no rocks, no twist. The dogs sit with me, curled at my feet in a glowing finger of sunlight. They may be the first ones to move when it happens. I'm surrounded by those I've taken care of and loved, and we're waiting.

Waiting ….

I'm not sure I'm ready this time.

ABOUT THE AUTHOR

GREG RODE

GREG RODE is the author of the *Sanctuary Chronicles* series (and a children's book he hasn't quite figured out what to do with yet). He lives in Cornelius, North Carolina with his family and two small dogs that would be of no use whatsoever when the zombies come. He used to live next to the golf course described in *Shotgun Finish*, but has moved twice since then. The zombies followed him anyway, which is a good thing since they keep him out of trouble. He is still not a very good golfer.

www.ingramcontent.com/pod-product-compliance
Lightning Source LLC
Chambersburg PA
CBHW022038240626
47154CB00007B/2465